THE ANGEL AND THE ARISTOCRAT

MERRY FARMER

THE ANGEL AND THE ARISTOCRAT

Cover design by Erin Dameron-Hill (the miracle-worker)

ASIN: B092KJ89BH

Paperback ISBN: 9798520704348

Click here for a complete list of other works by Merry Farmer.

If you'd like to be the first to learn about when the next books in the series come out and more, please sign up for my newsletter here: http://eepurl.com/RQ-KX

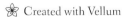 Created with Vellum

CHAPTER 1

*L*ady Angeline O'Shea was used to being afraid. She'd spent most of her life in a state of one kind of fear or another. Sometimes, it had been the fear that it would rain when she wanted to meet her wild cousins, Shannon, Marie, Colleen, and Chloe, and have a go on one of their new bicycles—and it always rained, because she lived in Ireland. Sometimes it had been the fear that her beloved father would succumb to his lengthy illness—and he had succumbed just six months before. And sometimes, it had simply been the fear that she would lose her embroidery needle in the cushions—and she usually did loose her needles, because needles were so small and slippery. Angeline always tried to put the best face on things, in spite of her fears, and so far, she considered herself an expert at smiling when her heart trembled.

But walking up to the grand front door of Fangfoss

Manor to join her old friends from finishing school at a lengthy house party instilled an entirely new kind of fear in Angeline that she wasn't certain she was ready for.

"What if they don't recognize me?" she whispered to her older brother, Lord Avery O'Shea, the new Earl of Carnlough, as he helped her down from the carriage the Countess of Fangfoss—who was formerly Miss Julia Twittingham, owner of the Twittingham Academy finishing school in London, where Angeline had spent two of the happiest years of her life—had sent to bring them to Fangfoss Manor from the train station in York.

Avery laughed good naturedly. "Of course, they'll recognize you, Angel. You haven't changed that much in five years."

"I feel as though I have," Angeline said under her breath. She waited on the gravel drive as Avery stepped around the carriage to speak with his valet, Mr. Crymble, who had made the trip with them, to make certain their traveling bags and the trunk of gowns Angeline had brought so that she could be ready for any social occasion were taken down by the driver and handed off to Miss Julia's—that was, the Countess of Fangfoss—oh, Angeline would never get used to calling Miss Julia anything but "Miss Julia"—footmen. "What if they are angry with me for not writing frequently enough?" she asked on.

"Haven't you been sending them each a letter a month for the past five years?" Avery asked over his shoulder, then gave a final instruction to Mr. Crymble before peeling away from the carriage. He offered his arm to Angeline to escort her up the terraced stairs to the front door, where the butler stood, ready to show them inside.

"Yes, but only one a month," Angeline said, as though it were a severe problem. "I should have sent them each a letter every week."

Avery sent her an indulgent smile—which was very Avery-like. He was as protective and affectionate as an older brother could be. "You were close with five of the other girls, weren't you?" he asked.

"Yes," Angeline said hesitantly. "Though I was especially friends with Lady Clementine Hammond and Miss Olive L'arbre."

"You would have spent all of your free time writing letters if you'd written to each of them every week," Avery argued. "And you had far more pressing matters to attend to."

"You are right on that score," Angeline said with a sigh.

In fact, nearly from the moment she'd left finishing school, after a very short season, during which she'd had a few prospects for husbands, but none that excited her, she'd been called back to Ireland when her father's health began to decline. She loved her father and had been more than happy to tend to him, she just hadn't expected that process to last for four, long years. In that time, she'd hardly had any society at all, let alone anything like the grand house party that Miss Julia had invited her and the others to attend. The entire purpose of the party was for each of them to find husbands, and frankly, Angeline was more than ready.

But, as with everything else, she was also frightened.

"What if none of the gentlemen Miss Julia has invited like me at all?" she asked Avery in a hushed voice as they stepped into the grand front hallway of Fangfoss Manor. "Or worse, what if the only ones who like me are gnarled and lascivious old men who are only interested in me as a brood mare."

"Angel!" Avery exclaimed. "How on earth do you know about such things?"

Angeline sent her brother a flat look as they waited where the butler told them to while he went to fetch their hostess. "Avery, we are no longer living in the Dark Ages, where women were held captive in towers to protect their virtue until such a time as their brother could marry them off to a man, sight unseen."

Avery looked horrified at the prospect. "You aren't telling me that you—" he gulped, "—have personal experience with...such things."

Angeline burst into laughter. She hated her laugh. It was too high and too exuberant. But she couldn't help it. "A lady does not need to be ruined to know about *such things* these days. I lived in London for two years, Avery. *London.* At a finishing school populated entirely by restless and marginally wicked young ladies. We shared our secrets and our knowledge. You can't expect me to have come out of a situation like that without at least *some* forbidden knowledge."

"I never understood why Mama sent you there in the first place," Avery said, looking rather sick.

Angeline giggled. "Because she wanted me to learn refinement and to catch the eye of a titled man of means."

"And instead, you learned all about *such things*." Avery shook his head.

"You're making it out to be much worse than it is," Angeline continued to giggle.

Blessedly, the conversation was interrupted as Miss Julia swept into the front hall with a bright smile of excitement. "Lady Angeline, how good to see you here at last," she said, drawing Angeline into a polite but warm hug. "I was beginning to worry."

"My apologies for delivering my sister late," Avery said, greeting Miss Julia with a gallant kiss of her hand. "We had some trouble with the passage from Ireland."

"I was so afraid that we wouldn't make it at all," Angeline said.

"Well, you're here now." Miss Julia squeezed Angeline's hand. "If your brother doesn't mind handling arrangements for your rooms and seeing to it that your things are delivered there, I can take you to the hyacinth parlor. Your friends are waiting for you there."

"Thank you so much, Miss Julia," Angeline said, her heart leaping with excitement. "I've been so anxious to see them again."

"It's Lady Fangfoss now, my dear," Miss Julia said with just a hint of impatience. "And your friends have been anxious for word of you as well."

They started down one of the halls that branched off from the entry hall. Angeline waved to Avery—who seemed pleased to see Angeline so happy—then nearly skipped her way at Miss Julia's side as they headed toward whatever the hyacinth parlor was.

"I'm certain your friends will be eager to tell you all about the opportunities and entertainments I've provided for you all this summer," Miss Julia explained. "I've spared no expense—well, my dear husband, Hubert, Lord Fangfoss, has spared no expense—to provide you ladies with everything you could possibly need to keep yourselves occupied. All of the diversions are designed to facilitate interactions with the gentlemen, of course. We have archery, badminton, and croquet perpetually available in the gardens, picnics and outings planned, and every Friday evening, we hold a dance of some sort, whether it is a ball or simply dancing in the conservatory. I trust you are prepared for tonight's dance?"

Angeline had almost forgotten it was Friday. "Yes, of course. I will be—oh!"

Her answer was cut short as she turned a corner into a parlor that was decorated all in shades of purple and pink, with paintings of hyacinths on the walls and bowls of hyacinths on the tables, even though it was out of season for them. But that was nothing to the sight of her two dearest friends, Clementine and Olive.

"Angel!" Clementine rose from the settee where she'd been drinking tea and conversing with Olive to rush across the room to her. "Look at you," she said, sweeping

Angeline with a wide-eyed look from head to toe. "You look so grown up and elegant."

Angeline laughed with pure joy and hugged Clementine back. "I don't feel particularly grown up or elegant." She switched to hugging Olive, giddier than she ever thought she'd be. "I feel as though I am Sleeping Beauty, awakened after sleeping for a hundred years, with no idea what has been going on in the world without me.

"Plenty has been going on," Clementine said, leading Angeline back to the settee where she and Olive had been taking their tea. "I've managed to find myself betrothed, for one."

And I've been busy with my research, for another," Olive said. "I completed my paper on rooflines and eaves in the Roman era, and Clementine and Charity and the others are trying to convince me to submit it to the Society of Archaeology journal."

"Trying? We *have* convinced her," Clementine said. "She's submitting the paper with the next post! But we want to hear how you've been doing, Angeline." She reached for Angeline's hand. "I was so sorry to hear about your father's death."

"Yes, how have you been, dear?" Olive asked, holding Angeline's other hand.

"I've been about as well as could be expected," Angeline sighed. "To be honest, after so many years of declining health, it was almost a blessing when Father died. He is in a much happier place now."

"But what about you?" Clementine asked. "Are you in a happier place."

"I am now," Angeline said, smiling at both of her friends. "I've missed you both so much. I've missed all of our group. And I've missed attending balls and musical events and pretty much anything where men are present."

"They're most certainly present here," Clementine said, a hint of mischief in her eyes.

"They are," Olive said, a bit warier. "I'm trying to avoid them."

"Oh, but why?" Angeline blinked innocently. "I simply cannot wait to meet the man for me and to fall in love."

Olive laughed. "You've been reading too many romantic novels, then."

"Haven't you?" Angeline asked.

"No, Olive has been busy reading books about the Ancient Romans and longing to go on archeological expeditions instead," Clementine said.

"Which reminds me," Angeline said, standing suddenly. "I brought that book from my father's library that you requested. I packed it near the top of my trunk. If I hurry, I can intercept Avery and the footmen before they carry it upstairs, and I can give it to you immediately."

"Angel, you don't have to do that," Olive called after her as Angeline darted toward the hallway. "I'd rather sit and visit with you first."

Angeline sped into the hall, turning to make a gesture to Olive indicating that it wouldn't take any time at all for her to fetch the book. The result was that she wasn't watching where she was going, though, and the gesture was large enough that as she turned to face forward again, her hand knocked against a tall vase of flowers placed on a table in the hallway. The vase was unbalanced to begin with, and as Angeline knocked it, the entire thing spilled right off the table, smashing on the marble floor.

Worst of all, the hallway wasn't empty. As the vase shattered, it spilled water, petals, and pollen all over the fine shoes and trousers of a man who was walking past the table. Angeline gasped and glanced up at the man—or rather, dragged her eyes slowly up his form, from his ruined shoes to his soaked trousers, his trim waist, broad chest, powerful arms, and glowering expression. He had beautiful, dark eyes that smoldered with anger, and thick, dark hair swept rakishly to one side. His lips were pressed in a firm line, and his strong jaw appeared to be clenched in frustration.

"Oh, dear," Angeline gasped, uncertain whether the words were for her clumsiness or the fact that she found the man devilishly handsome.

LORD RAFE MCALLISTER, MARQUESS OF ROTHBURY, hated house parties. He hated socializing in general, after all the trouble it had gotten him into in the last few months. He hated being away from home—either in the country or in London—and he hated sleeping in a strange bed. While he was at it, he decided that he hated Yorkshire, frivolity, and, oh, why not the entire female sex while he was at it?

"You cannot go on grousing like this about every tiny thing indefinitely," Hubert, Lord Fangfoss—who was a distant cousin of some sort that he'd forgotten about until the invitation to the blasted house party arrived—laughed as he took his shot at the billiard table, where several of the gentlemen were idling away their morning. "You're in the country, my lovely bride has provided you with a bevy of beautiful and accomplished young women to engage yourself to, and the weather has been uncommonly good for this time of year."

"That's true," the Marquess of Dorset said with a look that Rafe found entirely too teasing. "The weather has been uncommonly good." He shared a teasing glance with Mr. Phineas Prince, which Rafe could tell was entirely at his expense.

He knew Dorset in passing and Prince from all of his exploits printed in journals. Most gentlemen with a title or land who were within a decade of each other's age knew each other at least by name or from the House of Lords or previous house parties. Rafe had hoped that no one who knew him at all would be at the blasted house party. Not after the indignities he'd had to endure of late.

As if his thoughts were on display for all to see, one of the other gentlemen in the room, Viscount Wilton, sent him a sympathetic look and said, "Go easy on Rothbury.

His reputation has just been dragged through the mud and back again." He addressed the end of his comment to an impish, tow-headed boy who couldn't have been more than five, with whom he was playing some sort of string game that involved his fingers.

The others perked up. Fangfoss went so far as to straighten from where he'd been about to take a shot with his cue. "What's this about a muddy reputation?" He chuckled. "My bride didn't invite a rake into our house, did she?"

"No," Rafe said definitively, utterly out of sorts that the entire thing had come up at all.

"He was just thrown over by Lady Farrah Beauregard," Wilton said, smiling at the boy as he pulled the string off his fingers and slipped off the chair beside him.

The boy dashed toward the billiard table with a giggle, grabbed one of the balls, then darted out of the room before anyone could stop him.

"Oh, I say!" Fangfoss exclaimed, blinking in bafflement.

"Is he your son?" Rafe asked Wilton.

Wilton looked as confused as Fangfoss. "No, I assumed he belonged to Dorset."

Dorset was as perplexed as anyone else. "He's not mine. I thought he belonged to one of the servants of the house, perhaps."

"Certainly not." Fangfoss stood straighter. "We do not allow that sort of thing among our staff."

"Then whose is he?" Wilton asked.

None of them had answers. Rafe was more than happy for them to continue to discuss the matter, as it meant he could keep himself to himself, but that wasn't meant to be.

"What is this about you being thrown over by Lady Farrah Beauregard?" Fangfoss asked, leaning against the side of the billiard table, since the game was over.

Rafe sighed and rubbed a hand over his face. "It's a long and sordid story," he grumbled. He didn't feel as though he owed the entire story to his present company, but he didn't want to alienate himself entirely from his host and the other men he would have to spend the summer with, particularly not Wilton. "Lady Farrah and I became engaged at Christmas, as per the wishes of her family. I thought things were going well. I had yet to form any particular attachment to the lady, though I liked her well enough. At first."

"That doesn't sound particularly auspicious," Wilton said as he stood and moved to examine play at the billiard table.

"No," Rafe said in a dark tone. "The long and the short of it is that Lady Farrah decided she would rather canoodle with a barrister by the name of James Farrow than stay true to her vow to me."

"Bad luck, man," Prince said, focused on the billiard table.

"Yes, well, if only that had been the end of it." Rafe sighed. He was loath to explain, but too many expectant pairs of eyes were on him. "Word that Lady Farrah was compromised got out. Except, instead of the truth making the rounds, her family circulated the story that *I* was the one who besmirched her honor. Their reasoning was that Lady Farrah would be forced to abandon her lover to marry me in order to prevent a scandal."

"Which didn't happen?" Fangfoss asked.

"Quite the contrary," Rafe sighed. "Lady Farrah refused me, opting to spread the rumor that I had ruined her, then thrown her over. Now my reputation is suffering the consequences, and I've been snubbed and treated like a villain at every turn."

"My lovely bride must not have heard those stories," Fangfoss said. "We've been quite sheltered in our honeymoon bliss," he added with a self-satisfied laugh.

Rafe would have rolled his eyes, if he hadn't known how rude it would be.

"Begging your pardon, but why didn't you just demand to marry this Lady Farrah to spare everyone further scandal?" Wilton asked.

Rafe tried not to glower at the man. "Because she vanished, the chit. She and her lover."

"Have you thought to hire an investigator to go after her?" Dorset asked. "I know this man, a Mr. Arthur Gleason, who is devilishly good at finding people who have been misplaced."

"No, I have not thought to hire an investigator," Rafe said, trying desperately to keep his temper in check.

"Perhaps her family knows where she is?" Prince asked.

"They do not," Rafe snapped. He winced, instantly regretting his rudeness, but he'd been given every suggestion possible to remedy the situation already, and nothing had worked. "I beg your pardon, gentlemen. I'm afraid I am not in a fit mood for company." He nodded sharply, then turned to leave the room.

It was horrifically ungentlemanly of him, but Rafe knew that if he continued to attempt any kind of sociality whatsoever, he would likely make more enemies than friends. The situation with Lady Farrah was embarrassing at best and crippling at worst. Ladies were not the only ones who needed to be mindful of their reputations. Troubles arose for gentlemen who were deemed rakes or reprobates as well. And even though he had soured on the entire female sex, he did need to marry and produce an heir or two. The house party was as good a place as any to find a replacement bride, and if he was lucky, he could find a young woman of breeding who wouldn't—

His thoughts were cut short as a diminutive woman with strawberry-blonde hair dashed into the hall from one of the parlors, slammed her arm into a vase of flowers, and sent the whole thing, water and all, crashing to the floor in front of him. Water, pottery, and flowers spilled everywhere, including all over his new shoes and trousers. It was the very last straw, as far as Rafe was concerned, and he held his breath, clenching his jaw and fists, searching for exactly the right scathing reply to make to the careless woman.

At least, until she turned her bright green eyes and

porcelain-perfect face up to him. She was far and away the most beautiful woman he'd ever seen. For a moment, he couldn't breathe for a reason other than anger. But the magic of the moment was marred by the sudden pinch of terror that lit the woman's eyes.

"Oh, dear," she gulped, her beautiful face flushing. "Oh, I'm so sorry, so terribly sorry."

"It's...it's quite all right," Rafe mumbled, his voice not sounding like his own for some reason.

"No, no it isn't." The beautiful creature bit her lip and glanced around anxiously. She lunged forward, dropping to a crouch, and started to gather up the spilled flowers and some of the bits of the vase. "Silly me. I'm so clumsy sometimes. I should have been watching where I was going. And to think, I've only just arrived and already I'm causing problems."

She was Irish. Her voice had that unmistakable, musical lilt.

"Really, there's no need to fuss," Rafe said, gazing down at her.

"I think there is." She paused her frantic movements to glance up at him.

For a moment, Rafe's mind conjured the extremely wicked and inappropriate image of other things a woman as beautiful as this one could do from her current position on her knees in front of him. He was only human, after all, but his salacious thoughts were so much at odds with the woman's effusions of innocence that he cursed himself internally and crouched on the floor with her to help gather up the mess she'd made.

"It was a simple mistake," he said, pushing wet flowers to one side. The Fangfoss staff would be far better equipped to clean up than they were. "I'm certain you didn't mean it."

"I didn't," she said, blinking at him.

Rafe offered his hand to help her stand. It was the least he could do. Part of him wanted to smile at her to reassure her, but smiling seemed as far away as India to him at the moment. "Allow me to introduce myself," he said. "Lord Rafe McAllister, Marquess of Rothbury, at your service."

"Lady Angeline O'Shea," she replied with a smile so sweet and unfettered that he feared he would never be able to match it.

"Oh, my gracious, what has happened here?" They were interrupted by their hostess, Lady Fangfoss. "Oh, heavens. Reinhold! Come clean this up at once," she hollered, as though a footman would appear out of thin air. "Lady Angeline, Lord Rothbury, I'm so sorry. Let me fetch something to help you clean up."

"I am quite all right," Rafe said, backing away. He had the feeling if he didn't retreat immediately, he'd be drawn into some sort of social engagement that he didn't want to be a part of.

"What's happening out here?" a young lady asked, poking her head around the corner, followed by a second young lady.

"I was clumsy," Lady Angeline laughed. The sound was as beautiful and free as the hymns of angels, and Rafe found his heart—and his trousers—tightening. "But don't worry, I'll sort it out."

"You'd better leave me to sorting things out," Lady Fangfoss said. "You ladies go out and enjoy the sunshine. And perhaps Lord Rothbury will join you later?" she asked with a mischievous lift of her brow.

"What?" Rafe snapped. "Um, er, no thank you."

He turned and marched down the hall, fleeing from the tangle of ruined flowers, crushed pottery, and feelings of bliss that he'd nearly been mired in. He'd accepted the invitation to Fangfoss Manor as a way to hide from the scandal Lady Farrah had created and to, perhaps, dispassionately pick her replacement. He reached the corner and turned to steal a last, lingering look at Lady Angeline. He had not come to fall in love like a fool.

CHAPTER 2

*L*ord Rafe McAllister, Marquess of Rothbury. If ever there were someone or something for Angeline to be frightened of, he was it. She would never forget the way her heart trembled as she glanced up at him from the floor while cleaning up the mess she'd made. She would never forget the way her body tightened and trembled as well, but with an entirely different sort of emotion. She'd heard all about those women who were irresistibly drawn to men who frightened them or were harsh to them while at school, but never in a million years would she have dreamed she'd be one of them. And she wasn't.

Because as much as Lord Rafe had frightened her, something about him had touched her as well. Anger wasn't the only emotion she'd seen in his eyes. She'd seen a fair amount of sadness there too.

"Do you think he'll be here tonight?" she asked her

friend, Miss Melanie Pennypacker, as she and the rest of their group of friends walked toward the conservatory for that week's Friday night dance.

"Of course, he'll be here," Melanie laughed. Melanie was American, from Philadelphia, and had been sent to London for finishing school with the rest of them years ago in the hopes that she would find a titled husband, like so many other American "dollar princesses" who had invaded British shores. Angeline had no idea why she was still unmarried and still in England, but she was glad for it. "Miss Julia requires all of her houseguests to attend her scheduled events," Melanie went on.

"We've been informed that there is nae possible way for us to escape them, though I intend to try," Lady Raina Prince, another of Angeline's friends who she had just been reunited with said. "I've had enough of being snubbed and sniffed at by high society already. I will walk ye to the door, but ye cannae convince me to set foot in that ballroom."

"If you insist," Angeline said. She sympathized with her friend and the ill-treatment she'd received, but secretly she wished she could enjoy the evening with Raina.

"The dances are one thing," Raina went on, "but do ye ken she has theatrical events arranged for us to take part in as well?"

Melanie shuddered.

Angeline just laughed. "I never minded our theatric

endeavors in school," she said. "We were all fortunate enough to wear pretty costumes."

"Speak for yourself," Raina said. "She made me play a tree in that production of Macbeth that we were forced to suffer through. A tree! When I was the only actual Scot at the school!"

"I suppose she thought it would be too much on the nose for you to play Lady Macbeth," Melanie said.

"*Lady* Macbeth?" Raina balked. "I wanted the title role!"

The three of them laughed. Angeline clapped a hand over her mouth, once again hating the sound of her laughter.

As soon as they reached the door to the conservatory, Raina peeled away from them, backtracking as if she'd caught whiff of a horrible smell.

"This is as far as I go," she declared. "I wouldna set foot in that ballroom if my skirts were on fire and it contained the only water in the county."

"Suit yourself," Melanie laughed, glancing over her shoulder as Raina marched determinedly away. "We'll tell you all about it later."

Most of the gentlemen of the party were already assembled in the conservatory, watching the ladies arrive. Several of them took a keen interest in the newly-arrived duo. Angeline thought the gentlemen's attention was lovely, and there were some handsome men among them, but she turned this way and that, craning her neck, searching for Lord Rafe McAllister.

"Ladies, you all look charming," Miss Julia said, swishing over from the cluster of men where she'd been standing with her new husband to greet them. "I always knew that you would all grow into your looks."

Angeline exchanged an amused look with Melanie, who appeared to be having a hard time not laughing.

"Let me introduce you to some of our very special guests," Miss Julia went on, leading the three of them over to the group of men. "Gentlemen, may I introduce you to two of my most favorite former pupils? Lady Angeline O'Shea and Miss Melanie Pennypacker."

A short round of bowing and curtsies followed as versions of "How do you do?" were exchanged all around.

"And my dears," Miss Julia went on with an excited smile. "Please allow me to introduce the Duke of Cashingham, Lord Dorset, and Mr. Reginald Howard, a dear friend of my husband's."

Another round of bows and curtsies and versions of, "Lovely to meet you" followed that. Angeline's heart thrummed against her ribs, and she tried not to be overwhelmed by the amount of formality and protocol around her. She was a member of the Ascendency in Ireland, which meant she was used to society and polite gatherings, especially those with prominent English lords, but the whole thing made her head spin all the same. She'd learned everything she needed to know to deport herself at the Twittingham Academy, but she was so out of practice that it felt laughable.

"Oh, how lovely," Miss Julia went on. "The orchestra

has begun the first waltz. Perhaps you ladies would like to dance with these gentlemen?"

"That would be lovely," Melanie said, sending Angeline an amused look.

"If I might?" Lord Dorset offered his arm to Melanie.

"Certainly," Melanie said with a smile, then let herself be led off to the dance floor.

"Lady Angeline, would you do me the honor?" Cashingham offered his arm to Angeline.

"Why, thank you," Angeline said with as much of a smile as she could manage.

As Cashingham led her out to the center of the floor, Angeline looked sympathetically over her shoulder to Mr. Howard. The man wasn't exactly a sterling prize, what with his paunch, his receding hairline, and his slight, constant sniff, but Angeline felt rather like he had been handed the thin end of the wedge by not being paired up for the dance. Her friends would likely say she was being overly sympathetic to a man who didn't deserve it, though.

Angeline also glanced around for Lord Rothbury as Cashingham drew her into dance position as they waited out the opening strains of the waltz. Lord Rothbury had to be there at some point, as Melanie had implied. Angeline looked forward to seeing him again with an odd combination of hope and embarrassment. She didn't feel as though she'd properly apologized to him that afternoon. She hoped his shoes had dried out and that his trousers weren't ruined. But more than that, she longed to make him smile. He seemed too dour for a man who was so handsome.

The waltz began in earnest, and Cashingham led Angeline gracefully into the steps of the popular dance. That meant she was forced to turn her attention back to him. Unfortunately, she didn't have the first clue how to converse with a duke during a waltz.

"As I understand it," he began the conversation for her, sounding perfunctory at best, "Lady Fangfoss has arranged for this summer house party as a way to reunite some of her students."

He was a perfect gentleman, but Angeline still felt horrifically self-conscious. "Yes," she said bashfully. "We are her failed students, you see."

As soon as the words were out of her mouth, she yelped and snapped her mouth shut. Even if it was the truth, she shouldn't have been so blunt. She missed a step in her embarrassment as well, which caused the duke to step on her toes.

"My apologies," he stated drily, as if knowing it had been her fault.

"No, it was my fault, I can assure you," Angeline said, her face blazing hot. "I regret to say that I'm clumsy. And I often say all the wrong things. I haven't been out in company enough during these last few years. My father was dying, God rest his soul, and...." She pressed her lips shut, staring hard at Cashingham's shoulder so she wouldn't have to look in his eyes.

The man took his time answering. Finally, he

inclined his head the merest amount. "I forgive you. We all have our faults."

"I'm sure you don't." Angeline glanced up at him in awe. "You're a duke, after all. Dukes are...are perfect."

Again, her partner seemed to consider his words before answering, "I am not perfect. I doubt any man is." It wasn't anything as common as a moment of hesitation, but as if he was as careful with his words as he was with his expressions.

He was trying to make her feel better, but Angeline only felt worse. As they'd dressed for the dance, she and her friends had gossiped about the fact that Cashingham, a *duke*, was the ultimate prize for the young ladies invited to the house party. Who wouldn't want to marry a duke and become a duchess, after all? Especially since he was ever-so-handsome, with his stately pale good looks and his patrician nose. He seemed like a man born to rule, and knew it.

The more she danced with the man, however, the more Angeline got the impression he was quietly sizing her up, and judging her unworthy to be his duchess. Which was fine by her, because his censure caused her to miss her steps, and she didn't know what to say to him, and every moment of their dance made her feel as though she would be a terrible duchess.

"What do you think of Yorkshire so far?" Cashingham asked her politely after they'd made a few turns around the dance floor.

"I only just arrived this morning," Angeline

confessed, "but so far, I have found it quite—oh!" She gasped as—at last—she spotted Lord Rothbury stride into the room. "Lovely," she said, disconnected to anything else she'd been saying. "He's quite lovely. I mean—" she gulped and focused on Cashingham again, "—Yorkshire has been quite lovely so far."

The duke raised an imperious eyebrow at her, as if he knew full well where her thoughts had headed. Perhaps not specifically, as when he looked past her, his gaze didn't settle on any one man as the object of her sudden musings, but he seemed intelligent enough to guess.

"Of course I will be busy most days on my estate—Cashingham borders Fangfoss—but the countess sent me a full schedule for the party," Cashingham went on. "I was surprised to see she referred to some of the events as 'mandatory fun'?"

Angeline laughed. "Yes, well, Miss Julia—that is, Lady Fangfoss—used to hold Mandatory Fun events every Friday lunchtime at her academy."

The rest of the dance passed in a discussion of some of the things they'd all once been forced to do in the name of fun five years prior. Angeline found it much easier to talk to the duke once she'd decided he didn't see her as a marriage prospect. He was civil enough, and he was quite handsome, but they could both tell at once they weren't meant for each other.

Lord Rothbury, on the other hand, was a different story entirely. Cashingham must have caught on to who Angeline was staring at during the dance, because as soon as the music ended, rather than returning her to her friends, he did her the favor of escorting her over to Lord Rothbury.

"Rothbury, have you met the charming Lady Angeline O'Shea?" Cashingham asked once the three of them formed a small group.

Lord Rothbury cleared his throat. "We had the pleasure of meeting this morning."

"For which I apologize profusely," Angeline said. Cashingham's mouth twitched at her statement, which made Angeline realize how foolish she sounded. She fought to keep a pleasant smile in place, though, just as Miss Julia had taught them all to do when they were in school.

"Perhaps you wouldn't mind dancing with the lady so that she could apologize more?" Cashingham suggested with a nod for Lord Rothbury.

Lord Rothbury smiled, but it didn't count, because it wasn't a real smile. It was something tight and uncomfortable, as if he felt he had to. "I would be delighted," he said. He offered Angeline his arm as the orchestra swept into the next song.

Again, Angeline didn't know what to say as Lord Rothbury led her out to the dance floor, but for an entirely different reason from her speechlessness while dancing with Cashingham. She couldn't just stand there like a doll Lord Rothbury would be forced to hurl around the room, though.

"How are your shoes?" she asked in an embarrassed rush.

"They are quite well, thank you," Lord Rothbury said. He seemed to remember who he was speaking to and what the topic of conversation was, and went on with, "I expect they will make a full recovery. As will my trousers."

Something about that last statement made the otherwise handsome and dignified man blush. Angeline took that as a good sign. He wasn't angry with her, and he just might have a sense of humor lurking under all of his finery as well.

"I must apologize to your trousers for any discomfort I might have caused them," she went on, teasing him just a bit over his formality. "I can assure you that it was not my intent to alter their state at all, and I hope that the addition of a bit of dampness does not permanently interfere with their fit."

Lord Rothbury burst into a fit of coughing, though he managed to keep time to the steps of the waltz as he did. "Not at all," he said in a hoarse voice.

An awkward lull in the conversation followed. Angeline wasn't sure she minded, though. The silence gave her a chance to settle into their dance position and to attune herself more to the rhythm of the dance. It gave her a chance to observe Lord Rothbury as well. He truly was handsome, with his classically beautiful features and dark, fathomless eyes. And once again, she felt that sadness,

MERRY FARMER

that tension, that she'd noticed that morning in the hall. There was so much more to the man than met the eye. She wanted to discover all of his secrets, which was mad, really, since she'd only just met the man. But sometimes all that was needed was a heartbeat to know that you wanted to know someone. Her cousin, Chloe, would say it was written in the stars and that the two people must have had compatible astrological signs. Angeline wasn't so certain about that, but it had to be something.

"Are you enjoying Yorkshire so far?" she asked, taking a page out of Cashingham's book.

"My country estate is in Yorkshire," Lord Rothbury answered. "Though miles from here, right up at the very top of the county."

"Oh? How lucky you are to live in such a richly beautiful place," she said with a smile.

"My ancestors weren't so lucky," he went on, his expression dour. "They were constantly at war with the Scots."

Angeline suppressed a smile, wondering what Raina would say to that. "Do you have a house in London?" she asked, feeling more at ease and more confident in her ability to make light conversation.

"I do," he said with a nod. "In Berkley Square."

"How fashionable." Angeline brightened. "And do you spend much time there?"

"During the season," he answered. "When Parliament is in session."

He didn't say more, and his answer didn't give her

28

much to go on in terms of conversation. She had the odd feeling that he wanted to look at her, to study her face, perhaps, and memorize her for later, but his expression was determinedly neutral, and he didn't seem to be looking at anything at all as he moved her around the dance floor. Perhaps he was just shy. Mr. Darcy had been shy, and an entire book had been written about the misunderstandings that caused. Angeline made up her mind not to let any sort of misunderstanding exist between her and Lord Rothbury. Not that she was anywhere near as clever as Elizabeth Bennett. She still didn't feel as though she'd made amends to him properly for that afternoon, but the dance was exactly what they both needed to solidify a formal acquaintance. And once they were acquainted, anything could happen.

The waltz ended far too soon for her liking, even though their conversation had been sporadic at best, and when she indicated, Lord Rothbury walked her over to where Avery was standing at the side of the room. He graciously took his leave of her, perhaps lingering a bit too long over her hand, which suited Angeline perfectly.

"Who was that?" Avery asked with all the brotherly protectiveness he could muster once the two of them were standing alone.

"That was Lord Rafe McAllister, Marquess of Roth-bury," Angeline announced, as if claiming a victory.

Avery looked impressed for a moment. They both followed Lord Rothbury's progress across the room. He looked as though he were heading for the table where refreshments were set up, but before he could get close, Miss Julia intercepted him. She dragged him over to one of the other female guests and made introductions. Before Lord Rothbury knew it, he was walking out onto the dance floor with another partner.

"Poor devil," Avery laughed.

His laughter was short-lived, though. Miss Julia snagged the arm of Charity and pulled her over to where Angeline and Avery were standing.

"Lord Carnlough, have you met Lady Charity Manners yet?" she asked. Before either Avery or Charity could say anything, Miss Julia went on with, "I believe Charity would fancy a waltz right about now."

"Oh, I was just—" Charity glanced over her shoulder, then sent Angeline a look that begged for help.

"I would be delighted," Avery said, more than a little humor in his voice as he offered his arm to Charity. "It's what we're here for, after all."

Angeline sent Charity an apologetic look, then watched her and Avery make their way onto the dance floor. They took up a spot near Lord Rothbury, who Avery looked over with a stern, assessing look.

As if she were thinking whatever Avery was thinking, Miss Julia leaned closer to Angeline and said, "I saw you dancing with Lord Rothbury. You seemed quite taken with him."

"I felt the need to apologize for the incident with the flowers this morning," Angeline said, her face heating. "But yes, he is intriguing."

Miss Julia cleared her throat, the light of mischief in her eyes. "I was informed by my dear husband earlier about the unfortunate circumstances Lord Rothbury has just extracted himself from."

"Unfortunate circumstances?" Angeline's brow flew up, and she turned to Miss Julia, full of questions. "What unfortunate circumstances?"

"He was just thrown over by an ill-intentioned fiancée," Miss Julia whispered. "It was a bit of a bad business, as I understand," she went on. "Hubert would not give me all of the details, as he deemed them inappropriate for delicate ears, but I was given to understand that our Lord Rothbury has been grievously wronged."

"Oh, how sad." Angeline pressed a hand to her heart. "No wonder he has such a sadness about him."

"Sadness?" Miss Julia blinked. "I didn't notice that. I rather think he has a sort of anger in him that could use a good and sweet maiden to quell."

Angeline hummed, wondering if Miss Julia were referring to her. "That too, perhaps." She tilted her head to the side. "He is rather handsome."

"And he has a small fortune," Miss Julia whispered. "He's managed his family's estates well, but he also secretly invests, and he's very good at it."

"Is he?" Angeline was impressed that Lord Rothbury was an intelligent man, but money had never been her first consideration when it came to giving her heart away. Sometimes it was more of a deterrent than an attraction.

"I predict that you have a good chance of winning

Lord Rothbury's affections," Miss Julia went on, then gasped a bit and said, "I'm sorry, I see a gentleman who isn't dancing. We must remedy that situation immediately."

She grabbed Angeline's hand and tugged her off across the dance floor to the unfortunately unpartnered gentleman. Angeline had the feeling that no person standing singly around the edges of the conservatory would be safe from Miss Julia's matchmaking. She didn't mind being thrown at another man, though. Not when her mind was already made up. She had quite a bit more to learn about Lord Rothbury. He may or may not have been the right man for her. But if there was one thing she had determined already, it was that she would stop at nothing until she made the man smile.

CHAPTER 3

*R*afe never slept particularly well when he was under someone else's roof. It was something about the unfamiliar sounds and creaks. They always caught him off guard. He didn't like the idea that people he didn't know could creep into his room while he was asleep, even if it was just a maid come to light a fire. The unfamiliar unnerved him.

Which was probably, or so he told himself, the reason he felt so unnerved by Lady Angeline. She was as unfamiliar to him, as women went, as the strange bedroom he found himself in now. He couldn't stop thinking about her as he tossed and turned through the night, plumping the pillows behind him, flopping from one side to the other. He blamed his unease on everything but the truth that was staring him in the face. Lady Angeline had stooped to help pick up the flowers and pieces of vase that she'd been responsible for upsetting. She'd danced beautifully with him, smiled, and attempted to converse, even though he gave her so little to discuss. She radiated a sort of Irish sunshine that made his brain hurt.

Every woman Rafe had ever known—at least in a way that marked them as an eligible marriage prospect—had been cunning, vain, and more concerned with his fortune and title than himself. Perhaps he'd just been unlucky in the women he'd attracted, but that was the way things had been. Lady Farrah had seemed like the least offensive of the sparkling young things who had thrown themselves at him during the last season, but even she had proven herself to be fickle and selfish.

Lady Angeline was the opposite of all of those things. She was every bit as beautiful as Lady Farrah, though in an artless, unspoiled way. She was petite and shapely, and he could just imagine how perfectly her body would fit against his curled up in bed. But it wasn't carnal thoughts that left Rafe writhing and overstimulated—not to mention seriously considering taking himself in hand to relieve his relentless cockstand, even though he was a guest in someone else's house. It was the memory of the pure light in Lady Angeline's eyes, the kindness that radiated from her, and the mellifluous sound of her laugh.

By morning, Rafe was determined to cure himself of whatever disease it was that had poisoned his brain and made him unable to think of anything but Lady Angeline. As he headed downstairs to breakfast, dressed as impeccably as he could manage so that his outward appearance wouldn't reflect his inner turmoil, he determined that he would spend as much of the day as was possible with Lady Angeline. Proximity would prove that he was mistaken in all his positive assessments of the lady. She would inevitably do something to prove that he had made her into an angel in his head when, in fact, she was a harpy, like every other fortune-hunting miss.

"Oh, Lord Rothbury, don't you look handsome this morning," Lady Angeline greeted him the moment he walked into the large, bustling breakfast room, the light of the morning star in her eyes.

Rafe cleared his throat gruffly and gave her a stiff nod. "You are too kind, my lady," he mumbled, praying his face didn't go red. So much for familiarity breeding contempt. "Oh, and you look quite fetching yourself this morning," he added, cursing himself over the fact that it sounded like an afterthought.

In truth, Lady Angeline was stunning. Rafe knew nothing about women's fashion except how it made them look. The gown Lady Angeline wore was light and frothy, in a shade that reminded him of sunlight, and had bits of embroidery on it that looked like clovers. Of course, he had to stare particularly hard at her bodice to make them out, and only after the fact did he realize that made it appear as though he were staring at her breasts. It took every effort of will Rafe had not to huff and roll his eyes at himself before walking to the sideboard to fix himself a plate for breakfast.

The conversation at the table was already underway

by the time he had filled his plate and moved to find a seat.

"I'm just so uncertain," Lady Raina said, glancing out the window to one side. "Those clouds do not look particularly inviting."

Lady Raina had the pleasure of sitting beside Lady Angeline, who answered, "They don't look all that threatening to me."

Rafe tried to focus on his breakfast rather than hanging on whatever word Lady Angeline might say next.

"Now, now, ladies," Lady Fangfoss said from the foot of the table. "This morning's activity is already decided. We shall take a walk through my darling husband's extensive properties so that we might all get our exercise."

Dorset, who was seated to Rafe's left, chuckled. "It sounds to me as though someone has been reading a bit too much about these modern ideas of ladies and exercise."

Rafe shrugged. "Exercise improves one's health," he said. "Be it a lady or a gentleman."

Or perhaps he only thought so because it would be a delight to walk out with Lady Angeline, where they could put some distance between themselves and the others without being considered unchaperoned. Under circumstances like that, the woman was bound to say something that would put him off, and he could have his heart and mind to himself again.

Those thoughts were arrested when he had a

buttered crumpet halfway to his mouth as he glanced across the table to find Lord Carnlough glaring at him. It was all Rafe could do to continue eating without choking. A wave of incongruous guilt hit him, which he considered ridiculous. He'd done nothing at all to offend the man. He hadn't even spoken to him yet. What could possibly have put that dire expression on the young man's face?

But, of course, the answer was obvious. Carlnough must have seen him speaking with Lady Angeline at some point, or perhaps dancing with her the night before, and not approved. Rafe tried to avoid the man's stare by spending the rest of breakfast talking to Dorset, and to Fangfoss, once the man addressed him to ask about Rafe's investments in South Africa, but Carnlough was like a dog with a bone.

The matter came to a head when breakfast was finished and the ladies hurried off to fetch hats and shawls for the scheduled walk. Rafe lingered with some of the others in the patio garden at the back of the house, right off of the ballroom, waiting. That was where Carnlough found him, approaching like a lion tamer come to hold a vicious beast at bay.

"Carnlough," Rafe greeted him with a polite nod.

"Rothbury." The young man bowed as he came to a stop a few yards away, as if he shouldn't get too close to Rafe. He frowned, then launched straight into, "Sir, what are your intentions toward my sister?"

Rafe didn't know whether to be offended or amused

by the young man's directness. He also didn't have an honest answer for the question. So instead of answering, he said, "Forgive me, sir, have I done something to offend you?"

Carnlough let out a breath, dropped his head for a moment, then move in closer. "I saw the way my sister looked at you while the two of you were dancing last night," he said. "And then I asked around about you."

"You did?" Rafe couldn't think of any other reply.

Carnlough cleared his throat. "I regret to inform you, sir, that I cannot approve of any attachment between you and my sister."

Rafe wasn't an old man, not by anyone's assessment, but at that moment, he felt as though he had the weight of too much experience on his shoulders. Unlike Carn-lough, who was doing his duty toward his sister with a little too much ferocity. "What have I done to deserve this assessment, my lord?" he asked, addressing the young man as formally as the situation deserved.

Carnlough had the decency to look a bit embarrassed as he said, "It has come to my attention that you have recently ended an engagement to one Lady Farrah Beauregard."

Rafe would have sighed and rubbed his forehead in frustration, if he thought it would do any good.

"And it has further come to my attention," Carnlough went on, "that you did so after ruining the virtue of the lady in question."

It had only been months, but Rafe had the horrible,

sinking feeling that if he didn't do something to quell the rumors, they would follow him for the rest of his life. "You have been misinformed, sir," he said, switching to the less formal, more confrontational way Carnlough had addressed him in the first place. "The story you have been told is not only incorrect, the few correct details have been exaggerated to make me look like a villain on purpose."

That didn't seem to appease Carnlough at all. "Are you calling a lady a liar?"

The conversation wasn't going to go well anyhow, so Rafe rolled his shoulders slightly, then said, "I am calling the lady in question less than truthful."

Carnlough's back went straight. "Then, sir, that is all the more reason for you not to have anything to do with my sister. Do we understand each other?"

Rafe's mouth dropped open, but he wasn't certain what he wanted to say. He understood Carnlough, all right, but he also thought the young man was an overstepping young fool.

Fortunately for him, he didn't have to answer. A bundle of young ladies stepped through one of the ballroom's French doors, chattering up a storm, and looking lovely in their plumed hats and shawls. Lady Angeline was among them, and as soon as she spotted Rafe speaking with her brother, her face lit up so much that it compensated for the clouds in the sky above them.

"Isn't this delightful?" she asked, nearly skipping her way between them. "I had so hoped that the two of you would become friends. I was going to make the introductions myself, but it looks as though I won't have to now."

"Er...no," Rafe said, not wanting to disappoint her by pointing out that he and her brother were anything but friends.

"Angel, could I have a word with you?" Carnlough asked her in a low murmur.

Rafe's brow went up slightly at what he assumed was a nickname. "An angel" was exactly how he'd thought of Lady Angeline himself.

"Could it wait until after our walk?" Lady Angeline asked her brother in return with a pleading look. She darted her eyes sideways toward Rafe for the barest of moments, which shocked Rafe. The beautiful angel couldn't possibly actually want to spend time with him, could she?

"No, it cannot wait," Carnlough said, offering Lady Angeline his arm.

"Now, now," Lady Fangfoss said, sweeping in and breaking the siblings apart. "I haven't invited you all here so that brothers and sisters can entertain each other. Lord Rothbury is right here to escort Lady Angeline, and you, Lord Carnlough, would make a perfect companion for Miss Pennypacker. She's American, after all, and I hear the Americans are awfully fond of the Irish."

Carnlough sighed as Lady Fangfoss dragged him off. He sent Rafe a final, warning look as he went.

"I hope Avery wasn't bothering you too much," Lady Angeline said with an apologetic smile that made Rafe's blood run hot. "He feels responsible for me, you see. He feels responsible for a great many things, since our father passed away six months ago."

An unexpected knot formed in Rafe's throat. "I didn't know. I'm so sorry."

Lady Angeline clasped her hands together in front of her, weaving her gloved fingers together. She glanced down, sadness radiating from her, and said, "Papa was sick for years. That's why I returned to Ireland after finishing at Twittingham Academy instead of taking part in the season and finding a husband. Papa's illness was the wasting kind, and I became his nurse, tending to him and doing everything I could to make him comfortable as he declined."

Rafe's gut clenched. Spending time with Lady Angeline was supposed to drop the scales from his eyes and make him see her for who she truly was. The trouble was that Lady Angeline appeared to be every bit the angel he'd initially believed her to be.

"Come along, you two," Lady Fangfoss's overly happy voice called to them from the path that the rest of the couples she'd mashed together had started along. "We wouldn't want to leave you behind."

Rafe offered his arm with a somber look, as though scolded by the countess. Lady Angeline giggled lightly —a sound that went straight to his balls—and took his arm.

"You must have regretted all the balls and society events you missed," Rafe said, hoping to find a way to prompt Lady Angeline in to proving she actually was shallow.

Instead, Lady Angeline hummed and tilted her head to the side. "I missed my friends," she said carefully as they made their way to the start of the path. Lady Fangfoss shooed them along after the others, then doubled back to nudge a few other couples into the walk. "There were six of us who became particularly close in finishing school," Lady Angeline continued to explain. "We were devoted to each other then, and we are still dear friends now. I missed being able to support them in their triumphs and their defeats."

A woman who actually sought to support the others of her sex instead of cutting them down and undermining them at every turn? Rafe could hardly believe it. "But still," he went on, "you must have missed the gowns and the jewels, the box seats at the theater, trips to Paris, and all of the other accoutrements of society life."

"I've never been to Paris," she said a bit breathlessly, her eyes shining like emeralds. "I've heard it's beautiful and elegant. I long to sip coffee and eat *pain au chocolate* while looking out over the River Seine on a sparkling April afternoon."

Rafe was speechless. When Lady Farrah had talked of going to Paris, she'd prattled on endlessly about the modistes and shops and laughed about how much of his money she would spend. Not only had Lady Angeline not said the same, at her words, Rafe found himself imagining what it would be like to take her to the museums and tell her the little he knew about art, as if he were an expert. He wouldn't just buy her coffee and sweets, he would hire a chef for the day, rent a boat, and float idly along the Seine with her lounging in his arms as the spring sunlight warmed them and—

And what in God's name was he thinking? The purpose of the walk was for him to desire Lady Angeline *less*, not more.

"Do not misunderstand me, Lord Rothbury," Lady Angeline went on as they turned away from the more formal gardens at the back of the estate and ambled along a path that wound over hillsides filled with tall grass and wildflowers. The River Derwent flowed past in the distance to their left, while the site of the excavation of some Roman ruins that had recently been discovered stood on their right. "I enjoyed the time I was able to spend with Papa, even if it meant I wasn't able to go to Paris or attend balls in London."

"You did?" Rafe asked. "Even though you were nursing an invalid?"

Lady Angeline blinked in surprise. "That invalid was my father, and that time was all that I had left with him. Papa was a bit of a distant man when Avery and I were young, so these last few years were absolutely precious to me. I was able to love Papa and find love from him in a way neither of us would have had otherwise. No, I wasn't in society, but I believe those were the happiest years of my life, and even though he was ill, I believe they were the happiest for Papa as well."

God help him, Rafe was in over his head. His heart throbbed for Lady Angeline. His knees felt weak in the face of her beauty and her kindness. He wanted to weep with sentimentality at the way she spoke of her love for her father. Weep! Him! His own father was a drunken curmudgeon who hadn't so much as looked at him until he graduated from Oxford, and who had grumbled about him doing his duty—whatever that meant—until the day he died of a liver disease, making Rafe the marquess. Listening to Lady Angeline made Rafe long for things he'd never given a second thought to before. And it wasn't entirely a chaste love either, even though part of him said it should be. He wanted to tumble into bed with her, spread her under him, and give her so much pleasure that she came repeatedly, all while sighing his name.

"Lord Rothbury, are you quite all right?" she asked with a concerned look.

Rafe cleared his throat. "Er...yes, I'm fine."

"It's just that you've gone all red and splotchy," she said. "I haven't upset you with my story, have I? I can be a bit maudlin sometimes."

"No, it's not that at all," he mumbled.

As if the moment couldn't get any more like something out of a fairy story, a small, colorful butterfly landed on Lady Angeline's cheek, as though her face was a flower. Rafe thought his heart might explode in his chest.

Lady Angeline, on the other hand, yelped and brushed at her face, startled by something as light as a butterfly's kiss. She swatted at the poor thing until she

44

saw it was only a butterfly, then she burst into a laugh that was like heaven's bells. "Oh, dear," she said, clapping a hand to her mouth to smother her giggles.

"Allow me," Rafe said, reaching into the pocket of his jacket to take out a handkerchief so he could brush the dust from the butterfly's wings off of her porcelain cheek.

He'd no sooner brought the handkerchief out into the open than the same mysterious boy who had snatched a billiard ball from Hubert leapt out from behind him and snatched the handkerchief, then tore off into the grass before Rafe could react.

CHAPTER 4

*L*ord Rothbury had the most fascinating eyes. They were as dark as the earth after a good, hard rain and just as stormy. Angeline had a hard time holding onto her thoughts as she chattered on about inconsequential things while they walked because of those eyes. They were so full of emotion, even though he still wasn't smiling. Her mission to make the proud man smile was off to a terrible start. Here she was, talking about her father, instead of sharing stories of the silliness she and her friends had gotten up to in school, or telling tales of the things she'd seen at balls and other places Lord Rothbury would be familiar with. Five years of being away from society, and now she was completely out of practice at something as simple as talking to a gentleman.

But that was nothing compared to the way she overreacted when the butterfly landed on her cheek. She'd been startled was all, but for a moment, just a moment, she'd thought Lord Rothbury would smile at her giggling. That filled her with hope and made her feel as though she was just on the verge of victory when little Ewan dashed up from behind them and snatched Lord Rothbury's handkerchief.

"Oh!" she gasped, both amused and exasperated by the adorable little thief. "Ewan! Come back here! That handkerchief belongs to Lord Rothbury."

There was nothing for it but to pick up her skirts and chase after the boy, even though that meant leaving the path and plowing her way through the grass and uneven terrain of the meadow. Angeline didn't mind at all, though. Her victory with Lord Rothbury had her full of energy and excitement. She would have run to the ends of the earth, knowing she'd almost made him smile. It had her wondering how she would feel once she finally did manage the impossible task.

"Ewan, slow down," she shouted after the boy, giddy with happiness.

"Lady Angeline, you mustn't—" Lord Rothbury called after her, but apparently, he didn't know how to end his entreaty. "You'll twist your ankle or rip your gown," he called again.

He did have a point. The ground was decidedly bumpy under her feet, and the boots she'd donned that morning were more suited to walking on a sedate, even path than charging through a field. She was determined to return Lord Rothbury's handkerchief to him, though, even if it meant fighting the grass and the slight wind that had picked up as the clouds darkened and rolled overhead. Still, she clapped a hand to her hat, fisted her skirts in one hand, and trudged on.

"Ewan, darling, please slow down," she called, out of breath, as she reached the crest of the incline she'd just run up.

Ewan might have been young, but he was quicker than her and better suited for running through grass and wildflowers. He tore down the opposite side of the incline, heading for the line of other house party guests—which was now very much spread out along the path that skirted the river.

Lady Angeline stopped and pressed her free hand to her chest as she caught her breath. She spotted Lord Rothbury pushing toward her, even though the tall grass dragged at his trousers, but for the moment, she was more taken with the view from where she stood than anything else.

"Isn't it beautiful?" she gasped when Lord Rothbury finally came close, panting himself.

"It most certainly is," he said, something warm and heavy in his voice.

Lady Angeline wasn't certain what he was talking about, since he clearly hadn't taken in the full sight of the landscape yet. "I mean the view," she said. She marched back to him, grabbed his hand, and dragged him the rest of the way up to the crest of the small hill. "I know this isn't exactly a mountain, but it's like you can see the entire stretch of Yorkshire from here."

She turned to face it, one hand still on her hat as the wind picked up and swirled around them. The scene was perfectly idyllic. The meadow stretched away in all directions, green dotted with purple and white and mauve wildflowers. The river seemed restless as it wove along the edge of the scene to one side. The trees on its banks waved their boughs in the wind, and the scent of impending rain filled the air. In the other direction, the Roman excavation was less beautiful, but still intriguing with all its disturbed earth and tiny outbuildings.

"It's as though you can see all of time from this one spot," she said, the excitement of it all racing through her.

"It's captivating," Lord Rothbury agreed, though when Angeline turned her head to look at him, he was staring at her and not the scenery.

"Have you had a chance to visit the excavation site yet, Lord Rothbury?" she asked—mostly because the sudden fluttery feeling inside her left her uncertain as to what she should be saying.

"Call me Rafe," he blurted. A moment later, he blinked and shook his head slightly, then stuttered and said, "Er...that is...no, I have not. Not yet."

Call me Rafe? Angeline's breath caught in her throat. Calling a gentleman by his given name was an outrageous intimacy. It was something she never would have dared to do, not even with permission. But there was something about Lord Rothbury—Rafe—that begged for intimacy. It begged for affection and closeness, as if he'd never been given anything like it before.

"Are you—" She gulped, then started over. "Are you certain?"

"That I haven't seen the ruins yet?" he asked, a hint of teasing in his eyes. "Yes. Yes, I am."

"No, silly, I meant—"

Whatever she meant was irrelevant the moment she forgot about the wind and took her hand away from her head. The breeze was strong enough that it plucked her hat right off her head, hairpins and all, and sent it sailing across the meadow.

Angeline yelped, touching her hair. The style was hopelessly ruined, thanks to the force with which her hat had come off, but that was the least of her worries. With a laugh, she leapt after the hat, chasing it down the slope in the direction of the excavation.

Of course, there was a long distance between the crest of the slope and the excavation, and the wind was fierce enough to blow her hat out of her reach over and over. She slogged through the grass, leaping when she thought she might be able to reach it, then ended up laughing all over again when another gust carried it further away.

"I'll get it," Rafe called with manly gallantry, striding ahead of her through the grass and making a swipe for it just before another breeze picked up.

"Don't worry about crushing the brim," she called after him as he jogged through the wildflowers. His fine, masculine form was displayed well by a little running and reaching. At one point, he lifted his arms in such a way that the seat of his trousers was revealed. Angeline caught her breath at the firm shape of his bum, and her face went pink.

"Got it!" Rafe called at last, snatching her hat off of the grass where it'd finally landed.

Just as he turned toward her, the barest hints of a fledgling smile on his face at last, the skies opened up and rain began to pour down. That doused Rafe's smile in an instant, along with everything else. Angeline laughed. They should have seen the rain moving in, since they were out in the open, but hat shenanigans had distracted them. Now, they were still out in the open with buckets of rain coming down.

"We must get to shelter immediately," Rafe said in his serious voice of command, striding across the increasingly wet meadow toward her.

"Why?" Angeline asked with a teasing smile. "It's just a bit of rain."

"That's it precisely," Rafe said, reaching her and offering his arm. "It's raining. We wouldn't want you to get...wet." The way his voice fumbled on the last word was both curious and alluring.

"I'm already very wet indeed, *Rafe*," she said, sending him a cheeky look through her half-lowered lashes.

Rafe made a sound that Angeline found both intriguing and silly. They were both completely soaked in a matter of seconds, but something in the way Rafe looked reminded her more of fire than water.

"We should still take shelter," he said, hurrying her through the field toward the excavation site.

"I think you're right," she sighed, walking as fast as she could, which became harder and harder as her skirts grew sodden.

She thought she must have looked like a sight. The lightweight fabric of her day gown clung to her more and more as they walked, giving away everything beneath it. She only hoped that Rafe wouldn't hold it against her that her corset was as visible now as it would have been had she not been wearing a bodice at all, and that the tops of her breasts were visible along with it. Her skirt clung to her hips and legs as well, and by the time they reached one of the excavation's out buildings—a simple shed in which shovels and a few lanterns were stored—she felt embarrassingly exposed.

"Don't laugh at me," she warned him with a sheepish look as she hugged herself against shivers—not all of which were because of the cold. "I must look exceedingly silly to you right now."

"I can assure you, Lady Angeline, 'silly' is not the word I would use to describe you in your present condition," he said, his voice deep and pleasantly growly.

"What word would you use?" she asked, glancing up at him in the close confines of the shed.

He took a very long time to answer. There wasn't much light in the shed though two small windows in two opposing walls kept it from being completely dark, but there was enough for her to see his Adam's apple bob as he swallowed. She wanted to watch him swallow again. She could have studied the line of his neck all day, or his jaw, or the tight set of his lips. He had a lovely mouth, and she wasn't so innocent or inexperienced that she didn't want to kiss him. In fact, she was struck by the sudden interest in kissing him all over.

"Cold," he said at last.

"I beg your pardon?" Angeline blinked herself out of the wild thoughts that were making her anything but cold.

"You look cold," he said, then turned to the shelf at the back of the shed. "There are at least a dozen lanterns here. There must be matches to light them as well."

Angeline steadied her breath and her racing heart as Rafe searched for matches, then lit one of the lanterns. It didn't provide much warmth, but it did illuminate the shed. Illuminate it in such a way that made her wet and clingy gown all the more noticeable. Rafe glanced down at her, and his face pinched in such a way that hinted he was having second thoughts about the lantern.

"What were you and my brother talking about?" she asked, hoping it would distract him from their awkward situation and ease the pulsing tension between them. Although she wasn't entirely certain she wanted it to be eased fully.

"Er..." he began, looking sheepish. Angeline decided she loved the way he hesitated, loved the slightly awkward hitch that tempered the power he radiated. She smiled, which seemed to affect him somehow. "I won't be dishonest with you," he said in a different tone of voice. "Your brother doesn't want the two of us associating."

Angeline blinked, flinching back. "Whyever not? Avery doesn't even know you."

"He has heard rumors about me," Rafe confessed.

"Rumors?" Angeline's gut twisted with anxiety. She hadn't once thought to be afraid with Rafe by her side. Not through the entire ordeal that had landed them in the shed together. But now her heart trembled at the very idea of rumors.

Rafe let out a breath. "I was recently engaged, but that engagement is over," he said, rushing into the last half of his sentence.

"Oh." Angeline drew in a breath. That must have been why he was so sad. She was disappointed that his sadness was caused by another woman, though.

Until he said, "The lady in question decided she would rather marry her secret lover than me."

"Oh?" Angeline said, far more sympathetically.

"But the story that has made the rounds in society paints me as a villain of the worst sort," he finished.

"Those stories aren't true, though," she said, rather than asked. She didn't see how anything other than the highest praise could be true where Rafe was concerned. In the last twenty-four hours that she'd known him, he had proven himself to be a gentleman and a champion. He didn't feel like a blackguard either—which was a slightly flippant thing to say, but Angeline took great stock in the feelings that people gave her. She was convinced that Rafe was everything a gentleman should be.

And he'd been wronged.

"You poor thing," she said with a sentimental sigh, daring to rest one hand on his chest.

He sucked in a breath as though her touch were fire. "I am not after your pity," he snapped, then said, "I'm sorry, that didn't come out the way I intended it to."

"Not at all." Angeline shrugged to show that she hadn't taken the least bit of offense. "It sounds to me as though you've been through an upsetting time, so it is only natural that you have your defenses up. But I promise you, I don't think any less of you for your unfortunate circumstances. And if the lady in question was in love with another man, then you've done both her and yourself a great service by setting both of you free."

"There is the matter of the fact that I am being blamed for…for a great many things I didn't do," he said with a wince.

"I don't believe it," Angeline said. "I think you are a perfect gentleman, and you would never—"

Her words were cut off as he leaned into her, tilting her chin up with his free hand and closing his mouth over hers in a kiss. It was a perfect kiss—one that took her by surprise and drew the breath right out of her lungs. Rafe's mouth was soft and warm on hers, but the insistence and need behind the way his lips melded to hers and his tongue stroked across the seam of her lips, begging her to let him in, was intoxicating. She opened to him at once, sighing with delight as his tongue invaded her.

As quickly as the kiss had begun, it ended when Rafe pulled back. His hand that still held the lantern aloft trembled slightly. "I'm sorry," he said. "It was unforgivable for me to take such liberties, and—"

She didn't want to hear the rest of his apology. Careful of his arm and the hand holding the lantern, she threw her arms around his shoulders, lifted up to her toes, and gave him back every bit of passion that he'd given to her with their first kiss. She'd never truly kissed a man before—not like that—but she considered herself a fast learner. She brushed her tongue against his lips, and when he parted them in a gasp of surprise, she mirrored his earlier gesture and slipped her tongue along his.

A sort of shudder passed through him, and he set the lantern down. Angeline wasn't even certain where. All she knew was that his arms were around her a moment later, drawing her against his large, firm, warm body. Nothing had ever felt quite so wonderful in her life, and she sagged against him, surrendering herself fully. He slanted his mouth over hers again and again, kissing her jaw and the top of her neck as well.

"You're beautiful, my angel," he sighed, his every word as good as the touch of his lips. "I want you as I've never wanted anyone before."

"Oh," Angeline sighed. The sound was sensual and happy. She arched her neck to give him more space to kiss. She knew full well that she was being shameless and scandalous and wanton, but she didn't care. Not one bit. She also knew full well that the thing pressing against her belly was him, but that only thrilled her instead of frightening her. Every single bit of information she and her friends had whispered and giggled about in their Twittingham Academy dormitory at night rushed back to her at once, sending her mind reeling.

And she understood. She understood completely how a woman could let herself be ruined. She understood how irresistible it was to feel this way with a man and how she would have happily done everything he wanted her to do, right then and there, if he'd only ask. It was powerful, frightening knowledge to possess—not just in her mind, but in her body. But through that fright was a solid trust in Rafe and everything he meant to her.

"I think they dashed in here," someone's muffled voice sounded from outside the shed.

It was just enough of a warning for Angeline to pull out of Rafe's impassioned embrace and for Rafe to grab the lantern from the shelf where he'd set it. They were already wet and bedraggled, not to mention flushed from running, when the door to the shed flew open, so there was nothing at all to make Charity and Olive suspicious at the sight of them.

"There you are," Charity said with a relieved laugh. "We saw the two of you run into the ruins, but we didn't know which of the buildings you'd taken shelter in."

The two women crowded into the tight space of the

shed with them, shutting the door against the rain, which continued to pound.

"If it were me," Olive said, "I would have chosen to shelter in the building where they have bits of pottery and artifacts from the dig instead of where they store the shovels." She glanced around and sniffed.

"Lady Fangfoss ran back toward the house, saying she would send a small carriage around to collect her 'guests in distress', as she called it," Charity laughed. "So all we need to do is wait."

"And what were the two of you talking about?" Olive asked.

"Nothing," Angeline answered breathlessly. "I was saying that I don't mind the rain, because I'm Irish and we get quite a lot of it." Her heart thundered furiously against her chest as she peeked up at Rafe.

"Er...have either of you ladies been to Ireland?" Rafe asked awkwardly.

"No, not yet," Charity answered. "Though I would love to visit Lady Angeline at home someday."

"And I would love to have you," Angeline said, pretending nothing was out of the ordinary.

Though after what her friends had just interrupted, Angeline was beginning to wonder how long Ireland would be her home. She'd come to the house party to find a husband, after all, and, if she wasn't mistaken, the York-shire skies had just opened up and handed her the perfect one.

CHAPTER 5

*H*e was the very worst sort of cad imaginable. Rafe kept as quiet as possible in the shed as he and Angeline and her friends waited out the rain. When Lady Fangfoss's carriage came to fetch them, he said as little as possible and tried to be gallant as he helped the ladies into the carriage, then kept his distance from them so as not to drip on them during the ride home.

But as soon as they were all safely back at Fangfoss Manor, Angeline chattering away happily with her friends, as if Rafe hadn't just come within inches—a few rebellious, marginally painful inches that had distracted him through the entire wait for the carriage—of importuning her, Rafe took his leave of the ladies. Perhaps Angeline's spirits were a little higher than usual, but the remarkable woman in no way betrayed what had happened between them. He knew that he would be utterly incapable of pretending nonchalance if he stayed anywhere in her presence, though.

He tried to stay away from her for the rest of the day, which was somewhat easy, considering most of the guests had been drenched in the rain and spent the rest of the afternoon pressing the Fangfoss manor servants to their limit as one and all demanded towels and to have their fires tended to. The result was that most people were confined to their rooms until supper. Rafe offered to escort one of the older chaperones in to supper instead of Angeline, which meant he wouldn't be seated near her. It didn't stop him from losing the thread of the conversations he was supposed to be involved in and staring down the table at Angeline for most of the meal, though. Unfortunately, his attentions hadn't gone unnoticed. Though he didn't say anything, after supper, when the gentlemen retired to their own room, Carnlough glared at Rafe as though he knew exactly what had happened in the shed. It was enough for Rafe to decide to forego socializing with his peers and to head straight up to bed.

The next day was Sunday, which, again, made it easy to keep his distance from Angeline. The entire house party went in to York to attend Sunday services at Yorkminster, then lingered for a walk around the great cathedral and the town. Rafe caught Angeline craning her neck and searching here and there for something throughout the afternoon, but even though he couldn't guarantee she was searching for him, he stayed well out of sight all the same. He and some of the other gentlemen found themselves a cozy pub on a side street, where they knew the ladies wouldn't find them.

Rafe wasn't really interested in the conversation of his peers until Mr. Howard turned to him with a sudden, "And don't think we haven't all noticed that you already have your eye on one of the ladies."

Rafe shook himself out of his sullen thoughts and snapped straighter. "I beg your pardon?"

Howard snorted over his beer as he went to take a sip. "I've never seen a man so besotted with a woman so quickly."

"I'm sure I don't know what you're talking about," Rafe growled.

Dorset sent him a pitying look. "Come on, man, it's obvious. You haven't looked at any of the parade of ladies Lady Fangfoss has provided for us other than Lady Angeline O'Shea."

"Haven't I?" Rafe said, flustered. He tried to remember a single one of the other ladies' names so that he could make up a story about being interested in them. None came to mind.

"You haven't," Prince said, almost apologetically.

Rafe shrugged as if it didn't matter and took a swig of his pint. "I'm certain I have," he said in a way he hoped his peers would find absentminded.

Internally, he grimaced. He was such a love-sick fool that even men he barely knew could see it.

He determined right then and there that he would

block Angeline out of his mind. He would go about his business at the house party, assessing each of the young ladies based coldly on their merits in order to do his duty and find a marchioness. He would not let sentiment and the memory of the most perfect kiss he'd ever had cloud his judgement. He would not lie awake at night, staring up at the ceiling, cock throbbing, as he imagined Angeline as she'd looked in the rain, her gown clinging to the curve of her ample breasts, the shape of her hips, the way her eyelashes clumped together with moisture, making the emerald of her eyes sparkle. He would not think of her rosy lips or how they might feel against his once more, or pressed to his neck or over his beating heart, or circled around his cock.

"Blast it," he cursed, taking himself in hand and stroking at a punishing pace. He was a cad and a devil for thinking of Angeline in such a way, but if he didn't give himself at least some relief, he'd only lie awake all night, his thoughts swirling straight into the gutter. He didn't even last particularly long in his self-punishment, coming hard, then immediately falling into embarrassed worry about what the maids would think when they came to change the sheets the next day.

It was all some sort of blissful form of torture. No matter what he tried, he couldn't keep his heart from leaping in his chest every time he saw Angeline. He couldn't force himself to be dispassionate and not to land himself in another situation where he would just be disappointed when a lady failed to live up to expectations. Although, as they all gathered on the west lawn, where a tennis court was set up, late the next morning, as he watched Angeline laughing with her friends as they chose racquets and hit a few balls back and forth, it dawned on him that perhaps she wouldn't let him down the way others had.

He was on the verge of giving up his struggle to maintain his dignity and authority and rushing onto the tennis court to beg Angeline to let him be her doubles partner when the Fangfoss butler approached him holding a silver salver with a letter on it.

The butler cleared his throat, then said, "My lord, a letter has just arrived for you, and it is marked 'important'."

Rafe's brow went up, especially when he took the letter from the salver and saw that, indeed, it had the word "Important" scrawled on the front, along with the address, in a woman's looping handwriting. Curious, Rafe tore into the letter.

"*My dearest Rafe,*" it began, immediately giving Rafe a heavy feeling in his stomach. "*It seems I owe you the very deepest of apologies. I behaved foolishly and rashly in ending our engagement last month. I was caught up in sentiment that did not serve either of us, for which I apologize. I have ended my engagement to Mr. Farrow. I expect that you will greet this news with joy and relief, and it is my sincerest hope that we can continue on with our previous engagement as though nothing has happened. I should very much like to put this all behind us and go forward as we had intended. Yours, Farrah."*

Rafe gaped at the letter, astounded by Lady Farrah's audacity. How could the woman so cavalierly assume he would want to marry her again after the way she and her family had dragged his name through the mud. He huffed as he looked the letter over again, tempted to tear it into pieces and throw it in the fountain burbling away in the corner of the garden.

"Is something the matter?" Lord Wilton asked. He had been standing close to Rafe the whole time he read the letter, and he must have seen every one of Rafe's reactions.

Rafe humphed. "Only that the indomitable Lady Farrah Beauregard has informed me she has ended her engagement to that barrister, and that she wishes to continue on with me as though nothing had happened."

Fangfoss was standing close enough to hear Rafe's bitter explanation as well, possibly because Rafe had let his volume grow out of control in his incredulity. "I say, you wouldn't throw a lady as lovely as Lady O'Shea over for that harpy you were once engaged to, would you?"

Rafe didn't know whether to huff or laugh. Fangfoss, too, was among the legion of people who were certain he was pining for Angeline. "I have no interest in renewing my acquaintance with Lady Farrah," he said. "But you are mistaken if you believe I have any sort of attachment to Angeline."

He caught his slip immediately, and in spite of

desperately wanting to save face in front of his peers, he flushed. Calling a woman by her given name was tantamount to pinning a badge on her chest that said "Mine."

Wilton cleared his throat, trying not to humiliate Rafe by grinning too broadly. "You know, the O'Shea family are one of the most prominent families in the Ascendancy over in the north of Ireland. I believe her brother is an earl, which would make Lady Angeline eminently suitable for the role of Marchioness of Rothbury."

"And, come on, man," Fangfoss said with less grace and patience, moving close enough to elbow him in the arm. "She's pretty, you can't take your eyes off of her, and rumor has it that the two of you spent a great deal of unchaperoned time together in one of those sheds at the excavation site."

Rafe's face flushed even hotter. "Nothing happened," he lied. "We were merely trying to stay out of the rain."

Neither Wilton nor Fangfoss looked as though they believed him.

"Think of it this way," Wilton went on, shifting his stance slightly. "The house party has only just begun. No one expects you to make any declarations immediately. This Lady Farrah Beauregard can send all of the letters she wants, but she isn't here, and you aren't going to marry her. So why not simply take a few weeks to spend time with Lady Angeline to determine whether she is the right woman for you?"

Because he didn't want to be disappointed. Because

he didn't want to be humiliated by a woman again. Because he wasn't sure his heart could take it if Angeline turned out to be just as fickle and false as every other woman he'd known.

Except it wasn't every other woman, it was only Lady Farrah. And nothing about Angeline suggested anything but perfection to him. He wasn't risking humiliation if the events of the house party never made it past the boundaries of Fangfoss Manor. And his heart had recovered from disappointment before. It could do so once again.

"Very well," he sighed, tucking the letter from Lady Farrah into the inside pocket of his jacket, then tugging his jacket's hem as if donning battle armor. "I shall keep company with Lady Angeline, but only as a friend. This is not a declaration of intent," he told the other two men, then marched boldly forward to the tennis court.

"Oh, Lord Rothbury." Angeline noticed him immediately, as if she'd secretly had her eye on him the entire time he'd been standing watching her. "I'm so glad you're here. Clementine and I were hoping to play a game of mixed doubles, and I would be so pleased if you'd agree to be my partner."

The way she glanced up at him, those emerald eyes of hers shining, sunlight catching in her red-blonde hair, cheeks pink with promise, made it impossible for Rafe to say no. They made it impossible for him to walk comfortably as well.

66

"I would be delighted, my lady," he said with what he hoped was a chivalric bow.

"Lovely." Angeline's smile somehow managed to grow brighter. She grabbed Rafe's hand—something he felt, inexplicably, in his groin—and tugged him over to the side of the court, where a selection of tennis racquets was available. "Now, choose one of these, and I'll just have a word with Clementine about the rules of the game." She sent him a perfectly mischievous look before scampering off to where Lady Hammond was attempting to coerce one of the quieter gentlemen who had joined the house party, a Sir Nathaniel Radcliffe, to be her partner for the game.

Rafe picked up one of the racquets and tested its grip, glancing sideways at Angeline. The little minx was up to something, he was certain. She skipped over to Lady Hammond and whispered in her ear, all while glancing back at him, eyes sparkling. Rafe couldn't imagine what the woman was planning, and he couldn't account for the way it made his insides feel as bouncy as the tennis ball he picked up and hit with his upturned racquet a few times. He cleared his throat and frowned, telling himself he was a fool, absolutely determined not to so much as smile. Smiling would give away his feelings in an instant, and he was so unprepared for that that it was laughable.

"All right, Lord Rothbury," Angeline called from the court, gesturing for her to join him on the far side as Lady Hammond and Radcliffe took up positions on the near side. "We're ready to begin."

"I'm not certain I am," Rafe muttered to himself as he strode to the other side of the net to join Angeline.

She volleyed the ball back and forth to Lady Hammond a few times as Rafe approached. He refused to admit that he was walking slowly so that he might see Angeline in action. She had fine form, which surprised him, as tennis wasn't generally a sport for ladies. Then again, Lady Fangfoss appeared to be one of those who supported the latest medical findings about women's fitness, and Angeline had attended her school.

"Would you like to serve, Lord Rothbury?" Angeline asked once the practice volley was over. She offered him the tennis ball like Eve offering Adam the apple of sin.

Rafe swallowed hard, then took it from her, as big of a fool as Adam ever was. Angeline grinned from ear to ear, then stepped back into her place and took up a competitive, ready stance.

"Love all," Rafe said, only realizing after the fact what that must sound like. He cleared his throat, then served.

His tennis skills were subpar, but what he lacked in technique, he hoped he made up for in general athletic prowess. He kept fit as a point of pride, and chasing a ball around a court to smash it with a racquet shouldn't have been that hard. Except that he missed his first swing when Radcliffe returned the ball to their side.

"I've got it," Angeline called, hitting the ball back once he missed.

Rafe adjusted, tightening his grip on his racquet as

Lady Hammond returned it the second time. It was another easy shot that he should have managed to hit, but for the second time, Angeline raced to return the ball he missed. She kept going toward the net, and when Radcliffe reached to hit the ball back, she smashed it back over the net, winning them the first point.

"Good shot," Radcliffe panted, chasing after the ball.

"A very good shot indeed," Rafe complimented Angeline.

Angeline sent him a modest smile as she switched sides with him. "We used to play at Twittingham Academy. I believe I was rather good."

"Rather good" was an underestimation, as Rafe discovered in the next several minutes. Angeline was marvelous. She had no qualms about playing hard and working up a bit of a sweat. She was quick and light on her feet, winning them more than a few points as he struggled to keep up. But what astounded Rafe most of all was her seeming lack of vanity. Strands of her hair came out of the style she had it pinned in, damp patches showed up under the arms of her dress, and her shoes ended up scuffed and green, but she didn't seem to care. In fact, those imperfections made her look more beautiful in Rafe's eyes than any glittering debutante could.

"Are you not pleased with the progression of the game?" Angeline asked him after they won the first set and took a break to drink some of the lemonade Lady Fangfoss's footmen brought out for them.

Rafe blinked at the comment. "I'm very pleased," he said. "Why would you think otherwise?"

"You're not smiling," Angeline said. "Not even when I scored that remarkable point on serving against Mr. Radcliffe." She winked impishly.

Rafe's heart was in serious danger of beating right out of his chest. Angeline was sweet, she was good, and she had a devilish side to her as well. He didn't know how he would keep his head about him and his heart safe against her.

"I wasn't aware that smiling was a prerequisite to approval," he said, fighting to keep as stern an expression as possible.

"Of course it is," Angeline laughed. "And mark my words, I will make you smile if it is the last thing I ever do."

Rafe couldn't help himself. He shouldn't have taken up her challenge, but in spite of every instinct to the contrary, in spite of the way he'd been burned in the past, all he wanted to do was lay his heart at Angeline's feet. "I doubt that will happen," he said with a dour expression. "I only smile under the rarest of circumstances."

"Oh?" Angeline seemed energized by his comment rather than disappointed by it. "Then I shall have to work very hard indeed to create rare circumstances." She finished her lemonade, then turned and headed back to their side of the court. The glance she sent him over her shoulder was enough to strike Rafe dead with longing.

There was no point in denying it. His friends were

right, he was completely besotted with Angeline. It had happened far too quickly for his own good, and he still didn't trust his feelings for her. But Wilton had been correct to point out that they still had an entire summer to sort things. And the way things were going, all he would want to do all summer long was bask in the loveliness that was Angeline.

CHAPTER 6

The race was on. Angeline was determined to get Rafe to smile, even if it was the last thing she ever did. He didn't smile once during the tennis match, though. Not even when she deliberately made a ninny of herself by twirling and posing and adding dance moves to her playing. Clementine and Mr. Radcliffe were in stitches, but Rafe didn't smile once.

Rafe didn't smile when she made a little scene on her plate out of her vegetables during supper that night, then made certain he saw it. He didn't smile at all that week, not when they took another walk together and she told humorous stories of her cousins, Shannon, Marie, Colleen, and Chloe. He didn't smile the next week, when Miss Julia had them perform comedic scenes from Shakespeare and she played Olivia opposite Raina's Viola in a scene from *Twelfth Night*. He didn't even smile in church two Sundays later, when she sneezed in the middle of the long and boring sermon. None of their group could keep a straight face for the entire rest of the sermon, which ended with them being glared at as they left Yorkminster.

But the result of Angeline's efforts to make Rafe smile over the next several weeks was that she had ample opportunity to spend time with him, getting to know him and sketching his character. Not a day went by for four whole weeks in which they didn't spend at least some time with each other. Even on days when the gentlemen wandered off to partake in their own activities separately from the ladies. And with each conversation that they had about the Roman excavation on the property, the latest books that Miss Julia insisted everyone read, the goings on of Parliament, and a few spirited debates about The Irish Question, Angeline fell even more in love with Rafe. He was dour at times and guarded, but the more she spent time with him, drawing him out of his shell, the more she could see the good, noble, somewhat sad man that he was underneath his gruff exterior.

"Do you know, Lord Rothbury," she said one Tuesday afternoon in the fifth week of the house party, as the ladies all sat at easels, sketching the gentlemen, "I think this may be the very first time when your grave countenance is perfectly appropriate."

She couldn't tell if Rafe was entirely pleased with her teasing comment. She rather thought he wasn't. Or perhaps he simply wasn't pleased by the fact that Miss Julia had required all of the gentlemen to dress up in

Roman togas and to assume "Cesarian poses", as she'd called them, so that the ladies could sketch them against the backdrop of the excavation site. Though, frankly, the excavation site was mostly muddy holes in the ground, not sprawling Roman temple complexes or ruins of any kind. Like most of the other gentlemen—except Mr. Howard, for some reason—Rafe looked decidedly put out to be standing before a row of sketching ladies in nothing but a clumsily-tied bedsheet, leaning against a curtain rod that was meant to suggest a spear.

"There is nothing at all appropriate about this scenario, Lady Angeline," Rafe growled. His brow was already knit into a frown, but she fancied it dropped even further.

"Oh, I don't know, Lord Rothbury," she went on, tilting her head to one side, pencil on the rough sketch of her canvas. She drank in the sight of Rafe's powerful arms, which were pleasingly bared as part of his costume. She had more than a little peek at his chest as well, which was as aesthetically pleasing as any of the statues she'd seen in the British Museum. Rafe kept himself in fine form, if she did say so herself. The entire artistic exercise made the warm summer day even hotter than it would have been otherwise. "You would have made a very good Roman Senator."

She grinned at him, wondering if letting him see how transported she was by the sight of him would be the thing that finally made him smile. She wasn't sure it would, but his cheeks grew rather pink when she absentmindedly bit the end of her pencil while studying his bare calves as they stuck out from the bottom of his toga.

"I suppose that would all depend on which era of Roman history I was a senator for," Rafe said, entirely too seriously. "In the reign of Caesar Augustus, I think I would have done well. In the Emperor Caligula's time, however, I would likely have ended up with my head on a platter."

"Do you think so?" Angeline went on, adding a few more clumsy lines to her sketch. "I would have thought you'd have done quite well in Caligula's court. All that intrigue, all the naughtiness." She glanced up and met his eyes with a wicked look.

Rafe coughed for no reason whatsoever. "And what do you know of...Roman history?" he asked, his voice a bit hoarse.

"We studied it a bit at Twittingham Academy," Angeline said with pretend innocence. "And then some of us engaged in independent study once we were alone in our dormitory at night."

She thought her comment was fairly innocuous. All she'd meant was that Raina had secreted away some books from the library that detailed the depravities of Caligula's reign—books they knew full well ladies weren't supposed to look at. Rafe turned a particularly interesting shade of purple at her comment, though.

"Er...is that the sort of thing young ladies get up to at finishing school?" he asked in the oddest voice.

"What sort of things?" Angeline asked, blinking at him. "Do stay still, Lord Rothbury."

He had shifted in the strangest way, pulling his hips back so that his pose appeared more awkward than senatorial. He cleared his throat. "Nocturnal activities?" he suggested. "Between friends?"

Angeline cocked her head to one side. "Raina used to take books from the library that she shouldn't have," she said. "Books about the ancient world. We would read aloud to each other after curfew. Raina was particularly good at making dry academia sound interesting."

"Oh, oh, I see," Rafe said, letting out an enormous breath and looking mortified.

Angeline returned to her sketch, but paused with a sudden grin to ask, "What did you think I meant?"

"Um...er...I didn't...I assumed...."

"That we practiced kissing with each other?" Angeline asked, as casual as you please. "Well, we did that too."

She couldn't see his expression as she'd gone back to looking at her sketch, but Rafe made the most interesting sound, something like a strangled moan. Angeline made certain her face was hidden by her easel before grinning to the point of giggles. She would never understand men and their fascination with something as banal as friends kissing. As far as she was concerned, she would rather have kissed him a thousand times over than any of her friends. It absolutely was not the same.

"Ladies and gentlemen, I'm afraid we must cease our

artistic activities and return to the house," Miss Julia announced, interrupting them all. "It will take some time to walk back, and if we do not keep to our schedule, we will not be in time for supper tonight. So please do leave your drawings here, and I will make certain the Fangfoss staff pack everything up and transport it to the house."

"And what about us?" Mr. Phineas Prince asked, glancing down at his toga. "I'm not walking across York-shire dressed like this."

"The ladies can go on ahead while the gentlemen resume their normal attire," Miss Julia said.

"I suppose that means I will see you back at the house, Lord Rothbury," Angeline told Rafe with a smile.

"I suppose," Rafe said with his usual frown. He made a beeline for the outbuilding where the gentlemen had their clothes, his face still red.

Angeline giggled as she stepped away from her easel, making her way to Melanie so she could have a companion to walk back to the house with. Olive was still frantically sketching away, and Miss Julia looked as though she was about to scold her into leaving her drawing to return to the house. Angeline wasn't certain she wanted to be there for that.

"I saw you flirting away with Lord Rothbury, don't think I didn't," Melanie said with a teasing look. "And I heard what you said to him."

"You did?" Angeline's face heated, and she suppressed a giggle.

"You know what men think when you tell them

things like that about boarding house dormitories," Melanie said.

"That was the point," Angeline whispered, picking up her pace to put some distance between her and Melanie and the rest of the party. "I have been trying to get the man to smile for weeks now."

"I assume that's not all you've been trying to get him to do." Melanie arched one eyebrow.

Angeline sighed and hugged her friend's arm tightly. "Oh, Mel. I'm so in love with him. Lord Rothbury is everything I've always dreamed of in a man."

"Truly? You've dreamed of a gruff and grouchy curmudgeon who cannot be bothered to converse with anyone properly?" Melanie asked.

Angeline laughed. "He's been wronged, you know. By his former fiancée. He's merely shy now. But he's such a kind-hearted man underneath all his prickles. And as I've just discovered, he's quite fetching underneath all his clothes as well."

"Why, Angeline O'Shea, you're as bad as your cousins," Melanie laughed. She paused, then said, "Though I do think Miss Julia was unexpectedly wise to make the gentlemen pose in dishabille. It might just spur things on a bit."

"I certainly hope so," Angeline sighed. "Because I am quite certain that I want to marry the man."

"Are you?" Melanie's brow went up.

"Completely certain. In fact, I need to ask Avery to

arrange it immediately," Angeline said, filling with energy at the idea.

"Then you might want to ask him later rather than sooner," Melanie said. "From what I've observed, your brother isn't particularly keen on Lord Rothbury. The more time you give him to get used to the idea, the more likely you are to get him to agree to things."

"You know, I think you're right."

Angeline was so convinced of it that as soon as they reached the house and she was able to track down her brother—along with several of the other men who had somehow managed to avoid dressing in a sheet to pose for the ladies—she dragged him aside into one of the small parlors to force the issue.

"Avery, I will be blunt with you," she said, chin lifted, feeling confident in herself and what she wanted. "I would like to marry Lord Rothbury, and I wish for you to arrange it."

Avery gaped at her as though she'd expressed a wish to travel to the steppes of Asia to fight Genghis Khan. "No," he said. "Just, no."

Angeline's joy flopped to her feet. "No?"

"Did I not enunciate clearly?" Avery asked. "No."

Angeline pursed her lips and huffed through her nose. "Avery, that isn't fair of you. Lord Rothbury and I get along so well. Have you not seen the two of us spending so much time together these past four or five weeks?"

"I have, and you have not heeded my instructions to

stop and spend time with some of the other male guests at this house party," Avery said.

"There are no other male guests I wish to spend time with," Angeline argued. "Only Lord Rothbury. What possible objection could you have to your sister marrying a marquess?"

"I object to my sister marrying a rake of dubious repu- tation who has already ruined one woman he was engaged to," Avery said. His tone was harsh enough that Angeline flinched away from him. That made Avery wince and go one with, "I'm sorry to tell you the truth so bluntly, but there it is. The man is not worthy of you, Angel."

"In the first place," Angeline said with a sigh, "I know that Rafe has a broken engagement."

"Rafe?" Avery reacted as though she'd cursed.

"In the second place, if you disapprove so heartily of my marrying him, why have you not tried to keep us apart and prevent us from associating so closely for more than a month now?" Avery opened his mouth to answer, but before he could, Angeline rode over him with, "I think it is because, at heart, you approve of the match."

"I do not—" Avery stopped, pressing a hand to his forehead, and appearing to gather himself for a moment. When he glanced at Angeline again, his expression was tight. "Lord Rothbury was engaged to a Lady Farrah Beauregard."

"Yes, I know." Angeline kept her head tilted up,

telling herself she wouldn't be jealous of a woman who was no longer part of Rafe's life.

"Angel, he ruined her. They were caught in bed together," Avery said. Angeline's mouth dropped open. "And then he broke the engagement and refused to marry her."

The sizzling moment of hot and cold emotion that shot through Angeline's blood was replaced a moment later by incredulity. "But that doesn't make sense," she said. "Why would a man ruin a woman, then refuse to marry her when they were already engaged?"

Avery made an impatient sound. "I don't know, but that's what happened."

"And who told you this story?" she asked.

"It's all over Yorkshire and London," Avery said. "I wrote to some of my friends in London, and they confirmed the rumor."

"And did you ask Lord Rothbury himself?" Angeline demanded.

"I did," Rafe said, "but I did not find his answer satisfactory."

"Because he told you it was a lie, but you refused to believe him," Angeline assumed. "I knew it."

"Angel, you don't know anything," Avery said. That comment got her back up far enough, but then he went on with, "You will not marry Lord Rothbury."

"We'll just see about that, won't we?" she asked, then turned and stormed out of the room.

Her burst of defiance carried her all the way from

one end of the house to the other, but by the time she reached the hyacinth parlor, where her friends were, her spirits were flagging again.

"Oh dear, has something happened?" Clementine asked. "Has Lord Rothbury said something to upset you?"

"No," Angeline said with a mournful sniffle. "My horrible, dictatorial brother has."

Angeline flopped her way to the settee, and her friends instantly gathered around her.

"Can I wager a guess that he doesn't approve of Lord Rothbury and that he said you couldn't marry him?" Melanie said, wincing a bit. "I was the one who suggested she ask," Melanie told the others.

"That's precisely what happened," Angeline sighed. "Avery said no. Just no."

"I don't think that's very fair of him," Olive said. "What reason did he give?"

"Apparently, there is a rumor in London that Lord Rothbury ruined his former fiancée, Lady Farrah Beauregard, and after the fact, he refused to marry her."

"But that doesn't make any sense," Raina said, handing Angeline a cup of tea.

"That's what I told him," Angeline said, accepting the tea graciously. "The entire story must be wrong. I've come to know Lord Rothbury quite well in the last month, and the man isn't capable of anything like that."

"Isn't capable of ruining a woman or isn't capable of refusing to marry her once he has?" Clementine asked.

"Both," Angeline said with a burst of energy.

Clementine looked thoughtful for a moment, then said, "Perhaps you would be better off if he were capable of the first one, but not the second one."

Angeline blinked at her over the lip of her teacup as she took a sip.

"I think you have a point," Raina said, her eyes bright.

"What point?" Melanie asked, looking as though she wanted in on the fun.

Clementine moved to sit by Angeline's side. "How desperately do you want to marry Lord Rothbury."

"As desperately as it is possible to be," Angeline answered, nearly ashamed of the emotion in her voice.

"And how far would you be willing to go to force your brother's hand into letting you marry him?" Clementine asked on.

"As far as I can go," Angeline said. Giddy tendrils of excitement began to fill her insides. She had a feeling she knew what Clementine might have been suggesting.

"Oh, I see," Melanie said, her expression brightening. "I definitely see."

"What do you see?" Charity asked, coming to join the conversation.

"There's nothing for it," Melanie said with a shrug. "You're going to have to seduce Lord Rothbury, get him to ruin you, then force Avery to accept the marriage so that your reputation is not destroyed."

"Oh, my," Angeline said, both thrilled and terrified at the prospect.

But even that was a curiosity for her. She'd spent so much of her life being frightened by one thing or another, but in the past few weeks of keeping company with Rafe, she hadn't been afraid once. Rafe was too large and looming for her to be afraid of anything. He made her feel safe, even when he was being dour, and he made her feel cared for, even if he had yet to smile at her.

"I think I could do it," she said breathlessly, hardly believing herself.

"I think you could too," Melanie said with a shrug.

"I'm going to do it." Angeline put her teacup down and straightened.

"Excellent," Clementine said.

"How?" Angeline added, deflating slightly. "I've never seduced a man before. I've never done any of those things with a man before."

"It's not that difficult, trust me," Raina said with a mischievous look. "If he knows what he's doing, he'll guide you through most of it."

"And Lord Rothbury looks as though he knows what he's doing," Charity added with a wink.

"But how do I make it happen?" Angeline said. "The act itself is one thing, but how do I arrange for things to come together that way?"

"I have an idea," Melanie said, gathering them all in close.

Angeline had a feeling she was in for a night of wild excitement.

CHAPTER 7

*R*afe was fairly certain that he'd fallen through
the looking glass. Lady Fangfoss's house
party wasn't supposed to be such a diversion for him. He
was supposed to have been able to keep a clear head and
go about the business of choosing a replacement for Lady
Farrah to fill the role of Marchioness of Rothbury. He
was supposed to enjoy rest and the company of his fellow
gentlemen for a few weeks and then, hopefully, return
home early, his purpose for being there accomplished.

Instead, he'd ended up spending most of his time
being led around by the nose by Angeline. She had him
playing games, participating in dances, dressing up in
ridiculous costumes so that he could be sketched, and
even—perish the thought—singing a duet with her during
one of Lady Fangfoss's required evening concerts. What
in God's name was wrong with him? He would have to

make an appointment with his physician the moment he returned to London.

But no, that wasn't his problem, and he knew it. When Angeline left the aftermath of the concert early, claiming her head ached from all the singing and she would like to go to bed early, Rafe felt strangely bereft. He'd spent more than enough time with her in the last few weeks to determine that she was lovely, genuine, and most likely the perfect marchioness, so bidding her good-night and watching her hurry out of the room—and sending him a mischievous grin over her shoulder before she turned the corner, which was odd—shouldn't have left quite such a gaping hole in his heart. It did though, so much so that he found himself rubbing his chest.

"Is something the matter, old chap?" Lord Fangfoss asked, sidling up to Rafe as though he already knew the answer to the question.

"Er...no," Rafe said. "I am perfectly well, my lord." He tried an overly formal bow to see if that would get the man to go away.

It didn't.

"It's only that I saw the way you glanced after Lady Angeline just now," Fangfoss went on. "And I observed the perfect harmony between the two of you as you sang earlier." He raised an eyebrow significantly.

"Lady Angeline is by far the more accomplished singer," Rafe mumbled, searching for the line between too big of a compliment—which would give away his affections for certain—and too small of one—which would have the same effect, paradoxically. "If I sounded at all competent, it was only because she made me seem so."

"I think it's more than that," Fangfoss chuckled. "I do believe my bride will have another feather in her cap as far as matches at this party of hers goes."

"Quite," Rafe said, but only because it seemed like the most banal thing he could say.

"But what is this about another letter I hear you received this morning?" Fangfoss went on.

Rafe drew in a breath, trying in vain to gather the last of his patience. The staff at Fangfoss Manor had proven themselves to be accomplished gossips. "It is nothing," Rafe said through a clenched jaw.

"One would think that receiving a fourth letter from one's former fiancée in as many weeks is hardly nothing, sir," Fangfoss said, his eyes sparkling as though he enjoyed a bit of gossip too.

"I have not replied to any of them," Rafe said. "My association with Lady Farrah is over, whether she has come to terms with that or not. Now, if you will excuse me, my lord, I see that boy, Ewan, trying to get into the flower arrangements, and I feel it is my duty to tell him off."

Ewan—the little scamp seemed to be everywhere at the party, yet no one knew to whom he belonged—was indeed attempting to climb inside one of the potted palms in the conservatory, but Rafe had no interest in telling the boy off or joining him or anything. He used

Ewan as an excuse to get as far away from Lord Fangfoss as possible. Perhaps Ewan had the right idea, and he should hide in a potted fern for the rest of the night.

The trouble was, everything Fangfoss said was deeply disturbing to Rafe. It was alarming enough that Lady Farrah continued to write to him. Each letter included increasingly desperate pleas for him to forgive her, return to her arms, and to marry her as soon as possible. Reading between the lines, Rafe had to assume that the disagreeable woman was suffering the consequences of her lascivious and duplicitous actions and that she needed to marry as soon as possible to prevent the further ruin of her reputation. He'd tried to have pity on her for making foolish decisions, but it was damn near impossible to truly feel sorry for someone who had dragged him through the mud along with her. He could only hope that the timing of her love child would be such that society would realize it couldn't possibly be his.

The thought that he could be implicated in a bigger scandal soured Rafe's mood even more. He tried to join in a few conversations about politics, the situation in South Africa, and speculation about what mad-capped idea for their entertainment Lady Fangfoss would have for them all next, but even the company of his fellow gentlemen didn't ease his frustration. He kept finding himself glancing around, looking for Angeline, as if she would change her mind and come back to him. Er...that was... that she would come back to the conservatory to further enjoy the company of her friends.

Finally, he gave up. As soon as Wilton bowed out and was the first of the gentlemen to go up to bed, Rafe begged off as well. He was so eager to put the entire day behind him—except, perhaps, for singing with Angeline, which he would replay in his mind as many times as it took to ease his tension and enable him to fall asleep—and so he took the stairs two at a time, then strode down the hall to his bedroom at one corner of the house as though he were competing in a race.

He should have guessed that something was amiss from the moment he set foot in his room. The fire was lit at a low smolder, and the windows were open to let in the gentle night breeze. None of the lanterns that he usually asked the maid to keep lit so that he didn't have to grope around a dark and unfamiliar room upon entry were lit, though. He should have been more curious about that instead of removing his jacket, tossing it over the chair by the fire, loosening his tie, and sitting to remove his shoes. He should have registered the slight rustle from the area of the bed as something more than a mouse skittering across the opposite end of the room. He'd grown up in Yorkshire, so mice were as insignificant as gnats to him. He definitely should not have been so quick to peel out of his waistcoat and shirt, or to remove his trousers, and to drag himself over to his bed in just his drawers.

His last thought as he grabbed the corner of the bedclothes to throw them back and climb in bed was that the maid who had made the bed earlier in the day had done poor job of it and left the thing lumpy. That assessment flew right out the window, along with most of his sanity, when his motion to throw back the bedclothes revealed Angeline lying in his bed.

Angeline lying *naked* in his bed.

His mind cracked entirely, and he stared down at her, jaw dropping open in both shock and awe. The question of what the devil the mad woman was doing in his bed—naked—was superseded only by the feeling that she was far and away the most beautiful thing he'd ever seen in his life. Her petite form was absolute perfection. Her hips were shapely and her thighs were smooth and just plump enough that he thought he'd like to get his hands on them. Her breasts were gorgeous—round and soft with large nipples that he wanted in his mouth. Her skin glowed a perfect alabaster in the low light from the fireplace, and of course he couldn't help but feast his eyes on the sight of the thatch of hair between her legs, wondering what marvels he might find there if he went looking.

All of those thoughts were followed immediately by the realization that he was staring at her like a ravenous wolf. Also, that his cock had jumped to life and now strained against his drawers. Further, that he wore only his drawers, which were of the thinnest cotton and did very little to hide the state of his arousal. And finally, that Angeline was gaping at his erection with a combination of fear and fascination.

It took Rafe far, far longer than it should have to sweep the bedclothes back over Angeline to cover her and to turn away from her while asking, "Angeline, what in heaven's name are you doing here?" He strode away from the bed, searching frantically for his robe. For some horrific reason, he couldn't find it.

"I'm here to seduce you," Angeline said, almost as if declaring a triumph, and whisked the bedclothes away from her naked form once more.

"Seduce me?" Rafe blurted, his body flushing hot and his cock stiffening even more. "But...how? Why?"

"I would have thought the how would be obvious," Angeline said, a hint of disappointment in her voice. She shifted on the bed and sat up, her legs tucked under her. She did not, however, make any effort whatsoever to cover herself, even when she crossed her arms. The gesture only highlighted her lovely, perfect breasts. "Although I must confess, this entire seduction business is more complicated than I imagined it to be."

"More com—" Rafe didn't even bother to finish his incredulous question. And where was his blasted robe anyhow? Of all the times for it to go missing. He gave up his search, figuring the situation was already so far out of hand that him addressing Angeline while nothing but a thin layer of cotton separated his cock-stand from her view wasn't going to make it any worse than it already was. He walked to the side of the bed, keeping his distance—although, increasingly, his body and his heart told him that if the lady wanted to be seduced....

He shook his head. "You do realize that if we are discovered like this, your reputation will be completely and utterly ruined, and, in all likelihood, you will be shunned from all good society for the rest of your life."

"Yes, I do understand that." Her emerald eyes glittered as she pushed herself to her knees and scooted toward the side of the bed closest to him. "That is why we cannot be caught. My aim here is to be utterly debauched and thoroughly ruined beyond all repair by you tonight so that Avery will drop his stubborn refusal to consent to our marriage."

Rafe could only stand there and gape at her. There were so many layers of wrongness about everything she'd just said that he could barely comprehend it. She had deliberately come to his bed with the intention of him ruining her? As a ploy to convince her brother to let them marry?

He shut his mouth and blinked, raking her inviting body with a look before he could stop himself. She was right about the effectiveness of that ploy. Not even Lord Avery O'Shea, Earl of Carnlough would deny a marquess if he ruined his sister. She was also right about the need not to be caught. If no one but Avery ever knew he'd ruined her, Angeline could keep her reputation and still secure the right to marry. And perhaps most important of all—something Rafe realized with startling clarity, after weeks of muddying the waters with unnecessary angst and unfounded worries about Angeline's true character—he did want to marry her. How could he ever have been so stupid to think that he didn't? He'd known from the first moment, when she'd knelt at his feet to pick up the mess she'd caused instead of fetching a servant to do it, that she was the one for him.

All the same, he crossed his arms and stared at her scoldingly. "You know, there might have been another way for us to convince your brother to agree to a match between us," he said. "He's expressed his reservations to me as well, but I could have talked him out of those and made him see the benefits of the arrangement."

"Oh," Angeline said, sitting back on her heels. "I hadn't thought of that."

The picture that Angeline made, kneeling in his bed, her eyes downcast, biting her lip as she reconsidered the rashness of her actions—naked—was almost more than Rafe could bear. He wanted to do things to her—wicked things. He wanted to kiss every inch of her, learn every curve of her body. He wanted to taste every part of her and give her so much pleasure that she was dripping for him. He wanted to hear her cry out his name as he thrust inside of her, encompassed by her warmth.

"Oh!" she said in an entirely different tone once she glanced up at him again. Her cheeks pinked and her eyelashes fluttered as she caught her breath. Only then did Rafe realize he'd let every one of his thoughts show in the way he devoured her with his eyes. "Well," she began cautiously, threading her fingers together and glancing coyly up at him, "I don't suppose," her gaze dropped to his bulging drawers, "you might want to seduce me anyhow? Even if you plan to rationally and reasonably discuss the matter with my brother tomorrow? You know, for...fun?"

Rafe was absolutely certain of several things, all within the space of a fraction of a second after her question. He was certain that the two of them would have a long and satisfying life together, for one. And he was certain that they would end up with roughly a dozen children, because he had no intention of ever denying that naughty look of hers every time she turned it on him.

He plucked at the drawstring of his drawers, letting them sag open and his cock spring up. Angeline's eyes went straight to him, and she gasped in wonder. No man could ever have received such a stunningly perfect compliment. He let his drawers drop, then stepped out of them.

"Are you absolutely certain?" he asked, resting his hands on his hips and letting her ogle him all she wanted.

Angeline gulped, then glanced up at him. "If I am to understand the process correctly," she began hoarsely, "that goes inside of me?" She nodded to his erection.

"It does," Rafe said, working hard not to smile. He wasn't ready to give her that victory quite yet.

She frowned slightly, then asked, "How? It's so big."

Rafe's heart squeezed in his chest. Angeline didn't have the first clue how deeply she'd just complimented him. "Would you like to find out?" he said with a bit of a growl.

Angeline swallowed again, then nodded.

Rafe climbed onto the bed with her, deliberately

stalking her like a tiger. It was, arguably, silly and over-done, but his heart felt so full and light at that moment that he would have engaged in all the playacting the world had to offer if it meant he could live up to Ange-line's expectations. She gasped and flopped to her back as he positioned himself over her, gazing deep into her eyes with a look that he hoped communicated she was about to be ravished in every way. He nudged her legs apart a bit more forcefully than he should have, but her responding gasp and shiver was more than enough to tell him she was enjoying her seduction.

When he leaned in to slant his mouth over hers, kissing her as though there were no tomorrow, he knew that every risk they were taking, every wickedness they were guilty of, would be absolutely worth it. Angeline let him in immediately, humming deep in her throat and reaching up to close her arms around him. As he slipped his tongue against hers, putting everything he had into their kiss, she dug her fingertips into his back. More than that, she yanked his body down to cover hers, as if she knew exactly what she wanted.

"Have you done this before?" he asked, lifting his head up and arching one eyebrow.

"Certainly not," she answered breathlessly, staring at his kiss-swollen lips.

"You are far surer of yourself and far less reticent than I would have expected a virgin to be," he confessed, feeling the need to be honest with her.

"I've read more than my share of very dirty novels,"

she gasped, still staring at his mouth and wriggling under him. "And I've wanted to do this for a very long time."

Rafe didn't know whether to laugh or to be horrified. He opted for the former when Angeline surged up into him, capturing his mouth in a demanding kiss. Whatever novels she'd read, he was glad for them. He'd rather have her eager and expectant than terrified. He wouldn't question how she got her hands on dirty novels—the finishing school was probably to blame—but he was uncommonly glad his little angel had ended up in his bed before her curiosity led her to do something with someone else that she would have regretted.

"I shall endeavor to live up to the expectations set by your novels," Rafe growled, grasping her thigh and lifting her leg over his hip. He kissed her mouth again until all energy left her body and she relaxed into a puddle under him, then he began a voyage of kissing down her neck to her shoulder.

"Oh, this is lovely," she sighed, moving and shifting with him as he adjusted so that he could nuzzle, then lick and suckle her breasts. "Very—oh!—lovely indeed," she purred.

It was all Rafe could do to keep himself from turning into a ravening monster. Her breasts were everything he expected them to be, soft and responsive as he teased her nipples—one, then the other—to points. She tasted of heaven, and she shivered as he blew on the wetness he'd licked across one areola. Everything he gave her, she responded so openly and wildly. He kissed his way across her belly, teasing her navel as he did, then continued further toward the heart of her.

Rafe was so caught up in Angeline's responses that he nearly forgot how desperately he throbbed for her. He was reminded with a burst of urgency at the first taste of her wetness, though. The way Angeline gasped and cried out as he held her legs wide open and teased her with his tongue had him sweating and wildly ready to mate with her. The need to be inside of her consumed almost all of his thoughts, but he wanted to make her come first. He wanted to feel her explode with bliss and know that he had made it happen.

He didn't have to wait long, and part of him would have liked to lick and suck her longer. Her breathing hitched, turned fast and anxious, and then curled into a cry of pleasure that went straight to his soul as her body convulsed and throbbed against his mouth. He didn't want to wait for her to come down from her high of pleasure, particularly as he didn't know how much resistance her virginal body would put up at his invasion, so he shifted above her and pushed into her while she was still moaning in the final throes of her orgasm.

Her body did resist slightly, and she gasped in shock, but Rafe eased himself all the way into her, cooing calming words of reassurance as he held himself as still as he could and let her get used to him. As much as he regretted hurting her—though she seemed to recover quickly and move against him as if testing the new sensation of him inside of her—Rafe was smug over the fact that he was her first. He would be her last and only, if he had anything to say about it.

"You do fit," she whispered at last, flexing her hips against him.

He wanted to say something clever or loving, but his body was past the point of letting him. Instead, he moved slowly within her, careful not to overwhelm her. At least, at first. He couldn't fight his instincts for long, and when Angeline's sounds hinted to him that she was enjoying this new phase of their mating, he picked up his pace.

Somewhere in the back of his mind he thought that it might be wise for him to pull out before it was too late. The rest of him rejected that, though. Angeline was his, his angel, and he didn't want to waste any time fulfilling that in every way. He let himself go, thrusting until pleasure coalesced at the base of his spine and shot out of him like a glorious cannon, filling Angeline with his seed. He cried out with it, thrusting a few more times as every drop of him fused with every bit of her. She wasn't just his, with that, he was hers, forever. Nothing and no one could take that away from either of them now.

CHAPTER 8

*A*ngeline awoke to the sound of birds singing in the pre-dawn light, a gentle breeze blowing through the windows, rippling the curtains, and the steady rise and fall of Rafe's bare chest as she snuggled against his side. As soon as full wakefulness brought the memory of what they'd done the night before back to her, she grinned from ear to ear and let out a contented sigh.

She'd been thoroughly wicked, just like her cousins. She'd taken her friends' scandalous advice and been the minx she'd never dared to be. And it had been wonderful. She closed her eyes and stretched an arm over Rafe, wriggling in satisfaction as she inventoried all of the sore spots in her body. The whole thing hadn't been as big of a surprise as it could have been, thanks to the whispers and dirty books and even a few forbidden drawings she and her friends had shared in the dormitory of Twittingham Academy. At the same time, it had been a revelation.

Pictures and stories couldn't convey how heavenly it felt to have a man's hands on one's body. They couldn't describe the pulsing, swirling sensations of pleasure that having him kiss one's breasts, lick and suckle one's nipples, and do every manner of shattering things between one's legs could bring. The orgasm that had thundered through her was phenomenal, and all of that happened even before the two of them had been joined as one.

Yes, if that's what it took to secure Avery's consent to their marriage, then she was beyond glad that she'd had the daring to do it. She would insist that they have a short engagement so that she and Rafe could explore every manner of pleasure that the marriage bed brought with it.

Those thoughts lulled Angeline into a state of pure bliss that nearly had her drifting off into sweet dreams again—or else straddling Rafe and staring down at him until he woke up and repeated every one of their wicked actions from the night before. But a thump from the hallway left her gasping and reminded her that the other half of her plan, the half that would prevent her from truly being ruined and shunned from society, was to not be caught in bed with Rafe.

With regret in her heart, she leaned in and kissed Rafe's cheek lightly, then rolled out of bed as gently as she could, loathe to disturb him. She tiptoed across the room to where she'd left the nightgown and robe that she'd dashed through the halls wearing the night before. That had been an experience she didn't want to repeat soon. Creeping through the halls dressed for bed in the early morning, when only servants were awake, was one thing. Attempting to steal away to Rafe's room the night before, when most of the house party was still awake and could stumble across her at any moment, had taken years off her life. At least she'd been wise enough to change into a nightgown and robe so that she could have claimed to be looking for headache powder if anyone had stopped to ask her what she was up to.

As she straightened her nightgown around her and reached for her robe, her gaze fell on a small stack of letters sitting on the side table beside the fire. Angeline wouldn't have thought anything of it, but that the letters seemed to be addressed in the sort of loopy, spindly hand that could only be a woman's. Frowning, she finished donning her robe, tied the sash, then went over to see what the letters were. The one on top seemed to be the most recent, and when she opened it—Rafe wouldn't mind, after the night they'd just spent, they would soon be married anyhow—she scanned straight to the signature. Lady Farrah Beauregard.

Angeline gasped, touching a hand to her mouth as she scanned the contents of the letter. Lady Farrah wanted Rafe back. Rather desperately, it seemed. She didn't say so outrightly in the letter, but as far as Angeline knew, there was only one reason a woman would beg for a man to marry her, and for the marriage to happen as soon as possible.

She sat in the chair by the fire, grabbing the other

letters and opening them one by one, reading the story from the beginning. Everything came clear to her within the first two letters, particularly when she combined it with the cryptic things Avery had told her in refusing to allow Rafe to marry her. It appeared as though Rafe had broken his engagement to Lady Farrah after her reputation had been ruined. Ruined in the same way that her own reputation had potentially just been ruined.

Angeline bit her lip in consternation, staring down at the pile of open letters in her lap. Had she been a complete ninny and walked into the bed of a rake who routinely debauched innocent young maids? Would Rafe refuse to marry her now, as he'd refused to marry Lady Farrah? Had she done everything for nothing?

She looked at the letters again, trying to force herself to think clearly instead of casting herself in the role of some tragic heroine of a fairy tale. In the first letter, Lady Farrah had said she'd ended her engagement to another man. Not Rafe. She said that she wanted Rafe back because that relationship was over. That didn't mean Rafe was the one who ruined her.

"I suppose you have questions." Rafe's stern voice startled Angeline out of her thoughts.

She gasped, flinching enough to send the letters spilling to the floor. She slipped off the chair to gather them which, once again, resulted in her kneeling in front of him. Only, unlike the moment they'd met in the hallway downstairs, Rafe was now completely nude. Kneeling meant she was exactly at eye-level with a very

interesting part of him. A few of the other naughty illus-
trations her friends had shared around the dormitory and
giggled over rushed suddenly to her mind.

She realized she'd been staring too long at Rafe's
manly bits in front of her, remembered she had cause to
be concerned about his intentions toward her, and
instead of entertaining the scandalous thought that it
might be interesting to try what was in those pictures, she
stood and faced Rafe with a frown. "What are these all
about?" she asked, holding up the letters to him.

"As I'm sure you've deduced," Rafe said, taking the
letters from her hand with a scolding look that somehow
sent fire straight through her blood, "they are correspon-
dence from my former fiancée. The one who was false
with me, causing me to break the engagement. The one I
have not replied to in any way since receiving these."

"Oh." Angeline said, her shoulders dropping. She
wanted to trust Rafe, and mostly she did, but that tragic
fairy tale heroine part of her still buzzed. "So...you still
intend to marry me? Now that we've...." She nodded to
the bed.

"Of course I do, darling," he said, stepping into her
and drawing her into his arms. "Please don't doubt that
for a moment."

He kissed her tenderly, nibbling on her lower lip as
he did. It was wonderful and reassuring, and Angeline
ended up draping her arms over his shoulders and sighing
in contentment. "All right, then," she said, coming down
from her toes, which she'd had to rise to so that she was

tall enough for his kiss. "But you could smile when you say that."

"And ruin your contest to see if you can provoke me into a smile?" he said with a straight face, though his eyes were dancing. "Never." Angeline giggled, and he kissed her again before saying, "Now go. If you hurry, you can make it back to your room without anyone seeing you. I'll meet you downstairs for breakfast, during which we'll pretend that nothing at all has happened. Except for when I go to speak to your brother later."

Angeline made a sound of delight. She was about to get absolutely everything her heart desired. She felt as though she were dancing on air as she skittered out of Rafe's room, snuck back through the hallways to the corridor where the ladies had their guestrooms, and slipped back into her room, all without being seen. She couldn't wait to gather up her friends and tell them all about how triumphant their plan had been.

All of her joy and giddiness met a swift and crashing end the moment she made it downstairs. An unfamiliar, young woman with blonde hair and the bluest eyes Angeline had ever seen stood in the hallway, looking like a fashion plate. She was tall and slender, elegant and graceful, and at her first sight of Angeline, she turned up her nose with a derisive sneer.

"Oh," Angeline smiled, intending to greet the woman with as much warmth as possible. "Are you new to the house party? I'm Lady Angeline O'Shea." She started toward the woman with her hand outstretched.

"You're Irish," the woman said, as though pointing out Angeline was pestilential.

"I am," Angeline said, fighting to maintain her composure. "And you are?"

"Lady Farrah Beauregard."

Angeline's heart dropped to her stomach.

It dropped even farther when Lady Farrah went on to say, "I'm here to fetch my fiancé, the Marquess of Rothbury."

Angeline's jaw dropped next, but she didn't know what to say. Lady Farrah was every bit the sort of woman she would imagine Rafe wanting to marry. She had to work hard to remind herself that, in fact, he didn't want to marry her.

She was saved embarrassment as Miss Julia swept down the hall with a welcoming smile and said, "Lady Farrah, I'm so pleased that you could join us."

"I am not joining you, I am fetching my fiancé," Lady Farrah said, tilting her nose up. "I am not fond of contrivances intended to shuffle people together like a deck of cards."

Angeline's throat went tight with offense on Miss Julia's behalf. No wonder Rafe had thrown Lady Farrah over.

Except, had he? The woman was, there, calling herself his fiancée and saying she'd come to fetch him. It would have been extraordinarily bold of the woman to come all the way to Yorkshire and to invade someone else's party if she wasn't absolutely certain her errand would be a success. Rafe could have easily lied to her when he told her he hadn't replied to Lady Farrah. He could have assumed she wouldn't have a way to corroborate his story.

She shook her head, attempting to clear its dismal thoughts away and to trust her heart, which didn't think Rafe could possibly be untrue.

"Perhaps you would care to join us for breakfast?" Miss Julia went on, still trying to play the perfect hostess, though Angeline could see hints of the expression that had always come over her when her students were being particularly difficult.

"No, thank you," Lady Farrah said. "I am feeling unwell after my journey." She paused, glanced around her, then nodded to one of the parlors. "I will take tea in there while waiting for the marquess."

"Lady Farrah." As it turned out, Lady Farrah didn't have to wait long. Rafe reached the bottom of the stairs and stared at her. Angeline didn't like the way he took in the sight of Lady Farrah and all her elegance. She didn't like the way his face went pink, or the way he stood stock still as Lady Farrah marched up to him.

"There you are, Rothbury," Lady Farrah said, sweeping down the hall to him with a look that Angeline thought was decidedly relieved. "How fortunate that I don't have to scour this third-rate country estate for you."

Miss Julia gasped in offense.

"You always did have perfect timing," Lady Farrah

went on, reaching Rafe's side. "Except in certain circumstances."

Rafe merely gaped at her. "What are you doing here?" he asked after a long silence.

"I've come to bring you home," Lady Farrah said. "My father has already made all the arrangements for our wedding. He's procured a special license and everything. We are to be married tomorrow at St. Matthew's church."

Rafe continued to stare and blink at her for a moment. Then he did the most unforgiveable thing that Angeline could possibly imagine he could do. He smiled at Lady Farrah.

"Lady Farrah," he began. And yes, it was a bit of a condescending tone. And no, his smile wasn't even remotely warm or tender. But the whole thing was too much for Angeline.

Without waiting to hear the rest of the conversation, Angeline balled her fists at her sides and marched past the reunited couple and down the hall toward the breakfast room.

"Lady Angeline," Rafe attempted to call after her.

Angeline didn't listen. She knew she'd been a fool, she knew she'd taken a risk of astounding proportions, but she didn't need to linger in the hall to see the full proof of it.

"Is something wrong?" Charity asked as Angeline marched into the breakfast room, went straight to the sideboard, grabbed a fork and stabbed one of the long, thick sausages as hard as she could. Charity moved quickly to her side and lowered her voice to ask, "Did things not go as planned last night?"

Only a few people were already up and in the breakfast room. Angeline took her plate to the far corner of the table, where Melanie was already seated, and plunked herself down, shaking with frustration. Charity followed and took a seat on her other side.

"Everything went exactly to plan last night," Angeline whispered bitterly. "And then Lord Rothbury's fiancée showed up this morning, just now."

Melanie and Charity gaped at her.

"Hold on," Melanie said, leaning back and blinking rapidly. "The story I heard was that Lord Rothbury broke off the engagement because Lady Farrah had another lover."

Angeline's eyes went wide as she stared at her friend. "And have you had this information the entire time, but failed to mention it to me?"

Melanie looked duly sheepish. "I assumed you knew, since you and Lord Rothbury have grown so close."

Angeline deflated in her seat. "I only just found out." And it did make sense. A few more of the pieces painted by the letters fit into place. If she were a betting woman, she would have wagered that Lady Farrah had become engaged to this other lover after he made her some sort of promise that had swayed her from Rafe. That engagement to her lover was the other one that was broken, and if she were with child, it was the other man's, not Rafe's. But her family was desperate to save face, what with the special license and surprise wedding. She didn't think Rafe would consent to any of it, but that did not change the undeniable fact that, after five weeks of effort, Rafe had *smiled* at Lady Farrah as quick as you please. It was a small thing in the grander scheme of things, but it rankled her all the same. Or perhaps she was already rankled and Rafe's smile simply provided an anchor point for her frustration.

It didn't matter. Angeline's perfect picture of the way things would happen had been torn to pieces. Her story wouldn't unfold the way she'd imagined it would. Her moment of triumph was marred by Lady Farrah's arrival, and Rafe would need to spend his time dealing with her instead of arguing with Avery to give him her hand in marriage.

The whole thing left a sour taste in Angeline's mouth that stayed with her through breakfast—during which she ordered Rafe with a look when he finally entered the room to sit at the opposite end of the table and not speak to her—then through Miss Julia's explanation of the scenes from the comedy *Andria*, by the ancient Roman playwright Terence, that they would be performing that evening to continue on with the theme of Rome, and even after breakfast, when the ladies—all but Olive, who was off on her own adventure—left to equip themselves for a morning of target practice on the archery range in the garden. It was a beautiful day and the sun shone brightly, but Angeline was in no mood to feel sunny.

"And you say that he actually smiled at her?" Raina

asked as their group all aimed, then let their arrows fly toward the target. The moment they'd all released and the arrows from all five of them thudded into the targets —or into the ground, in Angeline's case—little Ewan dashed out into the grass to retrieve all of the arrows. "Ewan, do be careful," Raina called to the boy, then turned to the cluster of their friends.

"He smiled," Angeline said, jaw hurting from clenching it so much in the last few hours.

"Just like that?" Clementine asked, shrugging. "Without all the effort or trouble you've put into trying to get him to do the same thing?"

"Are you certain it was a real smile?" Melanie asked. "She doesn't look like the sort that anyone would smile at."

They all turned en masse to where Lady Farrah was sitting, her back straight, on one of the lawn chairs Miss Julia had had a footman bring out into the garden for her. Lady Farrah still managed to look elegant, even with a sour look on her face. She looked as though she believed her perspiration smelled like roses and the rest of them should be pouring her tea and breaking her biscuits up into pieces small enough for her to eat without soiling her gloves.

"She looks to me like the sort one would smile at simply to get them to go away," Clementine said.

Angeline let out a heavy breath. "I will concede that Rafe's smile was one of toleration and not as genuine as it might have been."

No sooner had she said that then Rafe stepped out through the conservatory door and onto the archery range. He searched for a moment, met Lady Farrah's eyes, and nodded to the woman. Angeline humphed in frustration. Then Rafe turned to her and started forward with an apologetic look. Angeline tilted her chin up, turned away, and marched back to her archery station. Her friends scattered back to their stations as well, though all of them kept a keen eye on what might happen next.

"Lady Angeline, may I speak with you?" Rafe asked.

"Not now," Angeline said. "I'm shooting things." She pulled back on her bowstring, brought the bow up all the way—which might have been the wrong way around from how she was supposed to fire an arrow, she never had been good at archery—and let the arrow fly. To her surprise, it landed near the center of her target with a satisfying thunk. With a triumphant grin, she turned to Rafe. "Would you care to be next?" she asked.

"I've no wish to shoot arrows right now," Rafe said impatiently.

"I meant as the target," Angeline said through a clenched jaw.

Rafe let out a frustrated breath and stared at her. "Do you not remember everything I said earlier?" he asked, trying to keep his voice down and glancing past her to her friends.

"I assumed those things were all rendered moot when your fiancée arrived and you *smiled* at her," Angeline said, stepping back to her quiver—which rested in a stand near her station—and took up another arrow.

To her surprise, rather than merely grumbling about her mood, Rafe said, "One thing you may not have learned about me yet, Lady Angeline, is that I do not stand for misunderstandings and the huffy moods they bring with them." He marched over and plucked the bow out of her hands, depositing it on the table behind her, then took her hand to drag her off to the far side of the garden. "You and I are going to have a talk, and we're going to have that talk *now*."

CHAPTER 9

So much for living a calm, rational life where every action led to another, rational action and no one got upset about things. Rafe almost couldn't believe the twists and turns his life had taken in the last eighteen hours, let alone the last five weeks, as he escorted Angeline to a sheltered corner of the garden, where they could have the conversation that was needed without being disturbed. By sweeping her into the hedge maze, he knew he was running a risk of causing a scandal. A gentleman shouldn't be alone with a lady before they were married, no matter what the circumstances. But seeing as he fully intended to be engaged to Angeline before the end of the day, he couldn't have cared less.

"Shall we dispense with the usual round of hurt feelings and accusations and leap right to the heart of the matter?" he asked once he had Angeline backed into one of the dead-ends near the beginning of the maze.

Angeline gasped and crossed her arms. "That was a terrible way to begin this conversation," she said, glaring at him. "I am fully entitled to hurt feelings, under the circumstances."

Rafe winced and took a step back. He rubbed a hand over his face. "You're right," he said. "I apologize. I was too harsh. But it was only because, after what you and I have shared, it wounds me as well to think that you would doubt me in any way."

Angeline blinked. "Oh!" Her expression softened. "That was a rather lovely way to say that." Her frustrated pout melted into an angelic smile, and she moved closer, smiling up at him.

Rafe's heart suddenly felt like an arrow that been fired wildly off course, spiraling and careening into who only knew where. "Allow me to try again," he said with overexaggerated gallantry.

"Yes, please do." Angeline nodded with mock solemnity.

Her teasing froze him before he could do more than open his mouth to go on. God, he loved her. He wasn't entirely certain when that had happened, but he was so deeply in love now that he wasn't sure he would ever be free of it, free of her. And dammit, he didn't want to be free of her. He wanted to be Angeline's forever.

He rethought what he was about to say. Instead of blurting something that would reasonably and rationally explain away Lady Farrah's appearance and his own callousness over the whole thing, he considered what

Angeline would want to hear. Once he'd decided on that, he dropped to one knee before her and took her hand.

"Dearest Angeline, I love you," he said, surprising even himself with his words.

Angeline gasped and clasped her free hand over her mouth.

"I think I began to fall in love with you from the first moment you ruined a perfectly decent pair of my shoes," he went on, feeling his heart lift, though he deliberately stopped himself from smiling along with his silly words. "I didn't want to fall in love, not after the thrashing my pride received though Lady Farrah's betrayal, but you forced me into it."

"Rafe," Angeline laughed, her face going pink and her emerald eyes sparkling, "I'm not entirely certain this choice of words is any better than your previous one." She couldn't keep the giggle out of her voice, which was lovely, as far as Rafe was concerned.

"You dragged me into love kicking and screaming, my darling," he went on, exaggerating his emotions even more. "You have turned me from a sane and rational marquess into a lovesick puppy who wants nothing more than to follow you to the ends of the earth and to curl up in your lap, slobbering and panting to be petted."

"Oh!" Angeline exclaimed, laughing so hard she snorted, and going redder than ever. "I know what that means now," she added with the sort of artlessness that made Rafe's heart—and other organs—throb for her.

"My dear," he said with a feigned sober look, "you

have hardly begun to know what that means. But I fully intend to educate you in all things wicked at our soonest possible convenience."

"Oh, dear," Angeline said breathlessly, fanning herself with her free hand. "I think I should like that very much. Do you think Lady Farrah's family would mind terribly if we appropriated that special license for ourselves?"

They were being silly, but Rafe took the opportunity of her mentioning Lady Farrah to grow serious. "My dearest, I was perfectly honest with you when I said I have no intention of entertaining Lady Farrah's mad notion of marrying her, and I did not, at any point, return her letters."

"I believe you," Angeline said, grasping his hands over hers with her free hand.

"Lady Farrah came here of her own volition, which was both bold and reckless on her behalf," Rafe went on. "I don't expect you to know the reasons she is so eager to get herself married, but—"

"She's with child, isn't she?" Angeline interrupted.

Rafe blinked, taken aback by hearing Angeline guess the truth. Then again, if she and her wicked little boarding school friends had read salacious books that had given Angeline foreknowledge of sex, then she probably knew more than most misses what the results of sex were.

"Yes," he said. "She told me as much earlier, after you stormed off."

"I was only upset because you *smiled* at her," Angeline said. "After I've spent all this time working so hard to tease you into a smile for me."

Rafe's brow shot up. "Did I?" he asked. He thought back on the situation and realized that he had. As soon as he realized his mistake, he felt terrible. But he also shook his head and said, "That wasn't a smile, that was a rictus of distaste for a woman who thinks far too highly of herself."

Angeline sent him a wry grin of her own. "It was a smile, Rafe. And you are a blackguard for dispensing one so cavalierly to a woman who did not deserve it."

"I am," he agreed, throwing her off-guard with his agreement. "And I promise that I will reserve all the rest of my real smiles for you for the rest of my life." He paused for effect, then added, "If you can pry them out of me."

Angeline's mouth dropped open, and she stared down at him, eyes sparkling, as if he were the wickedest villain that had ever roamed England. "You do drive a hard bargain, Lord Rothbury."

"So I've been told," he said. He drew in a breath, heart suddenly trembling, and asked, "Will you marry me, Angeline?"

He might have been slow to smile, but Angeline burst into the most beautiful smile he'd ever seen at his question. She squeezed her hands over his and said, "Yes, yes, of course, Rafe. And even though it was a given, since we've already done very naughty things, you've made me so happy by asking me outright. Yes, I'll marry you."

Rafe stood, and before he even realized he was doing it, smiled from ear to ear, as though the heavens had open and the angels had burst into song to congratulate one of their own. He leaned in to kiss Angeline, but before he could, she gasped and let out a cry of victory.

"A smile! A smile!" she said, laughing. "I've finally made you smile."

"You've done more than that," he said. "You've made me the happiest man in the world."

She opened her mouth, probably to tease him, but he silenced her with a powerful, tender kiss that came from the very core of his soul. He molded his mouth to hers, drinking in all of her sunshine and warmth, feeling as though he would never be able to stop smiling for the rest of his life. He brazenly sucked her tongue into his mouth and splayed his hands possessively on her sides, drawing her against him. She was so free and open with her kisses, and he was certain he would never grow tired of them, or of the sounds of pleasure she made as she circled her arms around him and rested her weight against him.

"I don't suppose we could get away with doing very naughty things in the hedge maze," she said with an impassioned sigh when Rafe paused to take a breath.

He laughed. "Certainly not. I may be willing to bend the rules of propriety and anticipate our vows later, if you deem it worth the risk—"

"I do, I do," she interrupted eagerly.

"—but not in a hedge maze in the middle of a Wednesday morning."

"No?" The look of impish disappointment Angeline gave him was enough to leave Rafe beaming even more.

"No, my dearest," he said, then kissed her lips gently. "Primarily because we have two major hurdles to leap over before we can race to the finish line."

"My brother," Angeline said, taking a half step back.

"And Lady Farrah," Rafe added with an arch of one eyebrow. "The woman is persistent. No, she is *desperate*," Rafe corrected himself. "And in a way that makes perfect sense. She has an extremely limited time to cover the mistake she made and to rescue her reputation in society. The fact that I want nothing to do with her machinations hasn't seemed to dampen her enthusiasm. She wants what she wants, and she isn't going to take no for an answer."

"But we're at a house party," Angeline said, the light of inspiration sparkling in her eyes. "Lady Farrah has come to precisely the right place to find a husband, and soon."

Rafe frowned. "Do you intend to convince her to marry someone else?"

"Do you think if she received a proposal that she'd accept it? No matter who it was from?" she asked in return.

Rafe stepped away from her and rubbed a hand over his chin to think about it. "I think she might be at a point where she would have to accept it," he said. "No matter who it was from. But if you attempt to match her with anyone who she doesn't think is worthy of her, she'll balk at the idea."

"Rafe, I have known Lady Farrah for all of five minutes, and I believe I can safely say that the woman doesn't think anyone is worthy of her. She can balk all she likes, but she's run out of choices."

"Then I'll leave the problem of Lady Farrah to you," Rafe said. "And in the meantime, I will handle the problem of your brother and securing his consent to our marriage myself."

"I know you can do it," Angeline said, grasping his hands and gazing up at him with complete faith. "You must be firm, but kind."

"I will be," Rafe insisted.

"You must be certain to express how much you love me and that you will not be able to live without me," she went on.

"I do love you, and I cannot live without you," he said, pulling her into his arms again.

"Avery is a man, so he will want to hear rational arguments as well," she continued. "So you must remind him you are a marquess. I seem to recall someone saying you are a man of means, so you must remind him of that as well."

Rafe's brow shot up. He'd somehow wooed and won Angeline, and she'd *forgotten* that he was as rich as Croesus? "I will enumerate everything," he said, then kissed her, simply because she was too lovely not to kiss.

"You must use all of your powers of persuasion with

my brother," she purred, staring at his lips as if willing him to kiss her again. "Avery will resist, but you must triumph. Tell him that I love you dearly, and if he does not allow me to marry you, I will never speak to him again."

"I will, my darling. I promise, I will." He gave the kiss she was looking for, savoring every moment. It was hard for him to believe that just a few short weeks ago, he had been depressed in spirit and doubtful about any chance he might have for future happiness. Now, he didn't know how he would ever stop feeling as though he were walking in the clouds.

"We must go," Angeline said at last, sighing. "You must find Avery, and I will set my plan for Lady Farrah in motion."

"Whatever you say, my heart."

They indulged in one more kiss—which became another one, and then another one—and when they could finally drag themselves away from each other, they exited the hedge maze as though they had every right in the world to be secreted in there together.

Angeline veered off once they reached the archery field to have a word with Lady Farrah—who Rafe determinedly didn't even look at—while he headed back into the house in search of Lord Carnlough. For all Angeline's advice and planning, he had a much simpler way to raise the question of their marriage, one he was certain O'Shea wouldn't say no to.

He found Carnlough with a few of the other

gentlemen in the billiard room and asked to speak to him alone.

"Dear me," Mr. Howard said, standing straighter and snorting like a boob. "I know what this conversation is all about. You've been nabbed, haven't you, Rothbury." The odious man laughed as though Rafe had stepped in dog mess.

"We'll just see about that," Carnlough said, clearing his throat and handing off his billiard cue to Wilton.

Carnlough fell into step with Rafe as they left the room to search for the closest unoccupied parlor to have their conversation in. "If this is about my sister, my lord, then you know my thoughts on the matter."

"I do," Rafe said. He paused as they located a suitable room and stepped inside, making their way to one of the windows so they wouldn't be overheard by anyone passing in the hallway.

"I hear that Lady Farrah Beauregard has joined the house party," Carnlough said with a mildly hostile look.

"I did not invite her," Rafe said. "I have told her I am not interested in renewing our suit. Forgive me for being blunt, but the woman means nothing to me."

"And my sister does?" Carnlough asked.

"Your sister means everything to me," Rafe said, clasping his hands behind his back.

"My opinion about the match hasn't changed," Carnlough said, "I refuse—"

"I bedded your sister last night," Rafe interrupted

him. "And I intend to do it again as much and as frequently as possible."

Carnlough stared at him, his mouth hanging open, his eyes bulging.

"But to prove my honorable intentions toward her," Rafe went on, "I will agree to marry her as quickly as possible, this weekend, if that suits you."

Carnlough shut his mouth and shook his head. "How do you propose to just marry her without all the proper licenses or banns being read or what have you?"

"I'll obtain whatever license is necessary to make it happen immediately," Rafe said, grinning inwardly at how flummoxed Carnlough was, but also knowing the man would capitulate without a fight. To ensure as much, he cheekily added, "That way, if I have an heir in nine months, no one will be the wiser. Oh, and your sister wanted me to inform you that she loves me, and if you do not allow her to marry me, she will never speak to you again."

Carnlough's shoulders dropped, and he let out a heavy breath. "That certainly sounds like Angel." He narrowed his eyes at Rafe for a moment, then shrugged and shook his head. "The two of you have tied things up nicely without my involvement at all," he said. "What's the point of having a chaperone for a house party if I'm left out of the entire process?"

"You get to enjoy a summer living at someone else's leisure," Rafe said with a grin. He could tell he'd won

Avery over, though he would have to put some effort into solidifying the friendship in the coming weeks.

"Then I guess, as Francis, my valet, was just telling me the other day, it's about time that I had some fun." Carnlough smiled.

Rafe raised one eyebrow. "Your valet told you that?"

Carnlough stepped closer, resting a hand on Rafe's shoulder. "You're going to be family soon, so I can let you in on the secret. Frank isn't just my valet, he's my and Angel's half-cousin. The O'Shea family has been wicked for generations now, as Aunt Nora proved twenty-five years ago."

"I see," Rafe laughed. He shouldn't have been surprised. He'd noticed Frank Crymble speaking a little too freely with Carnlough to be just a valet, and now that he thought about it, there was a definite family resemblance there. "Thanks for letting me into the secret. Now, if you will excuse me, Angeline has said she has a plan to get rid of Lady Farrah, and if you ask me, we both need to prepare ourselves."

"Jesus, Mary, and Joseph," Carnlough sighed, his accent coming out particularly strongly. "We're going to need to do more than prepare, we're going to have to pray."

CHAPTER 10

*I*n order to maintain what she claimed was authenticity—though Angeline had her doubts on that score—Miss Julia had insisted they stage that Wednesday's dramatics in a hastily-constructed outdoor theater at the corner of the rose garden. That meant that the entire thing had to be staged before supper rather than after, which meant Angeline had hardly any time to plan a scheme to get rid of Lady Farrah.

"The woman is mercenary, but she's desperate," Angeline told Olive as they applied their stage make-up in a tent that had been set up to serve as the ladies' dressing room behind the dais where the play would be performed. "She's barely spoken to anyone since arriving this morning, and she refuses to leave unless Rafe goes with her, which he absolutely will not do."

"I take it that Lord Rothbury has a decided reason to

stay?" Melanie asked, coming up to the mirror beside her and Olive, raising one eyebrow at Angeline's reflection.

Angeline broke into giggles, her face heating so much that she wouldn't need rouge for the performance. She turned away from the table and faced her friends. "Rafe proposed to me in the most romantic and glorious and scandalous way in the hedge maze this morning."

"That's wonderful for you," Olive said.

Melanie smiled, but crossed her arms and stared pointedly at Angeline, turning her smile into a bit of a smirk. "He didn't propose *too* scandalously, I hope."

"Oh, no," Angeline waved off her friend's concern. "The truly scandalous part was last night. It was the truly wonderful part too."

"You didn't," Olive gasped.

"Of course, I did," Angeline replied with pretend haughtiness. She then burst into giggles. "And it was glorious. Every expectation I had was exceeded. I recommend that the two of you find yourself a man to thoroughly bed you as quickly as possible."

Melanie laughed out loud, then clapped a hand over her mouth, looking particularly guilty, and turned away.

For a moment, Angeline was tempted to ask if her American friend had already landed herself in a scandalous position. Angeline hadn't noticed her paying special attention to any one of the male house party guests. In fact, she thought she'd spotted Melanie speaking with Avery's valet more often than anyone else. But the secrets of her friends' romances were less important at the moment than convincing Lady Farrah to go away and never darken Rafe's doorstep again.

"I suppose, since she is desperate, the only effective way to convince Lady Farrah to give up her pursuit of Rafe would be if she found herself engaged to someone else," Angeline said, turning back to the mirror to finish her make-up.

"But who?" Olive asked. "If the woman is as arrogant as we've all seen her to be, and if she has her heart set on a marquess, anyone lower than a duke would never do for her."

Angeline snapped straight and glanced from Olive to Melanie. "The duke," she said. "Cashingham. Lady Farrah would most certainly throw Rafe over for him."

"But I have serious doubts about whether Cashingham would consider engaging himself to a woman who only just arrived mere hours after meeting her," Melanie said. "No one is that much of an idiot."

"Well, Mr. Howard might be," Melanie said with a smirk.

"Mr. Howard would definitely be foolish enough to engage himself to any woman who expressed an actual interest in him," Angeline agreed. "Especially one as beautiful and well-connected as Lady Farrah. It's only a pity that—"

Angeline stopped, her mouth hanging open. They couldn't possibly pull a prank so horrible on Lady Farrah, could they? There was no possible chance that Mr. Howard would be able to play his part, let alone agree to subterfuge. Unless he knew what prize he stood to win if he played along.

"What if we had Mr. Howard *pretend* he was the duke?" Angeline asked.

"Have him pretend?" Olive looked at Angeline as though she'd gone mad.

"He's playing the part of Simo in the play," Angeline reasoned. "We could tell him we've decided to modernize the setting of Terence's comedy to reflect our current situation and that we're calling Simo a duke. Mr. Howard has been so enamored of his part that he'll strut around pretending he's a duke all evening. And I believe Lady Farrah would succumb to his advances out of sheer desperation, once they were made."

"But what will happen when she finds out he isn't a duke?" Melanie asked. "She'll cry off, saying she agreed to marriage under false pretenses."

"Will she say that when she realizes Mr. Howard is worth over a hundred thousand a year?"

The other two looked suddenly convinced of the idea. The three of them exchanged smiles.

"It's definitely worth the attempt," Olive said.

"Then let's put the plan into motion," Angeline said. "I will fetch Lady Farrah and convince her to join the theatrics. You two find Mr. Howard and tell him Lady Farrah's plight as generally as possible, and convince him to propose as soon as the curtain falls."

"You do realize this is sheer madness," Melanie said

as the three of them headed out of the ladies' tent to begin their missions.

"Of course, it is." Angeline smiled. "But that is what house parties are for."

The three of them shared a laugh, then went on their ways. Angeline wasn't certain she should have been wandering back up to the house dressed like a Roman housewife, but the circumstances required boldness.

No sooner did she set foot in the house when she encountered Rafe. Immediately, her heart lifted, and she ran to him.

"Darling," she said, nearly throwing herself into his arms and lifting to her toes for a quick kiss. The kiss left a bit of her lip rouge on his lips, but that only warmed her heart. "Did you speak to Avery?"

"I did," Rafe reported with one of the smiles she had worked so hard to drag from him. "And I am pleased to report that he has given his consent."

Angeline practically squealed with glee. She threw her arms over his shoulders and would have jumped into his arms like a child if she thought she was capable of it in her current state of dress.

"I've insisted we marry with all haste," Rafe went on, "to prove my seriousness. Your brother agreed, and he has plans to announce our engagement at the end of this ridiculous comedy Lady Fangfoss is insisting you all make fools of yourselves over."

"Oh, Rafe, that is simply lovely." Angeline kissed him one more time. "But I have my end of the bargain to uphold. I must find Lady Farrah at once. With any luck, ours won't be the only engagement announced at the end of the play."

"I beg your pardon?" Rafe stared at her as though she'd grown another head.

"You'll see," Angeline said, then dashed off in search of Lady Farrah.

She found Lady Farrah ensconced in the hyacinth parlor, frowning over a book and holding a teacup that looked as though she had forgotten about entirely. The woman glanced up at Angeline with a peevish look as soon as she burst into the room, but that look soon transformed.

"Lady Farrah, you must come at once," Angeline said, employing every bit of acting prowess she'd learned in her time at Twittingham Academy. "We are short one actress for a very important part in *Andria*, and we need you to play it."

"I will not," Lady Farrah said, tilting her chin up and putting down her book and teacup. "Theatrics are for children and whores."

Angeline ignored her, dashing to the settee and grabbing Lady Farrah's hand to help her to stand. "You must come," she insisted. "The duke himself requested that you play the part of Glycerium." Lady Farrah didn't need to know that, while Glycerium was spoken of frequently throughout the play, she never once actually appeared on stage.

"The *duke*, you say?" Lady Farrah's entire attitude

changed in an instant. "There's a duke at this house party?"

"There is," Angeline said. "And he's been ever so anxious to find a wife." She managed to lead Lady Farrah out to the hallway, then decided to take an enormous gamble. "He hasn't been pleased by any of the ladies in attendance at the party so far, but he noticed you this morning and declared that you were the bride for him." It was silly, it was outlandish, and it was wildly improbable, but if Lady Farrah was as vain and as desperate as Angeline thought she was, and if she and her friends could manage to keep Lady Farrah dizzy until it was too late, perhaps there was a chance the whole mad plan could succeed.

"Oh, my." Lady Farrah touched a hand to her belly, then seemed to realize what she'd done and lifted it to her heart. "A duke who fancied me at first sight." They turned into the conservatory, heading for the doors that would lead outside. Lady Farrah blinked. "The duke of what?" she asked.

Angeline felt their plan slipping. "Um, the Duke of Howard?" she suggested, hoping she didn't sound too daft.

"Howard," Lady Farrah whispered the name. "Howard. Howard. Why does that name sound familiar?"

Angeline swallowed. "Because it belongs to a duke?"

Lady Farrah didn't answer her ridiculous assumption. Angeline made certain there wasn't time. She grabbed hold of Lady Farrah's hand and rushed her across the yard to the ladies' tent behind the stage. Once they were there, she and her friends rushed to change the woman out of her afternoon dress and into one of the costume togas. Lady Farrah fussed and frowned the whole time, but, miraculously, allowed herself to be swept into the drama.

"How will I memorize my lines so quickly?" she asked as Angeline and the others pulled her away from the make-up table—where she'd spent an inordinate amount of time staring at her reflection and primping—toward the tent's flap.

"We're all performing with script in hand," Melanie told her. "Since none of us has time to learn so many lines so quickly."

"Oh, I see," Lady Farrah glanced at her reflection one final time before they stepped out of the tent and into the space between the ladies' tent and the gentlemen's tent behind the dais.

Fortunately for everyone concerned, Mr. Howard had just stepped out of the gentlemen's tent in all his regal, Roman attire.

"That's him," Angeline whispered to Lady Farrah.

She couldn't have planned the moment better if she'd had a month to work on it. Lady Farrah stepped up to Mr. Howard and went straight into the most elegant curtsy Angeline had ever seen.

"Your grace," Lady Farrah said with enough defer-ence to address the Emperor of Japan.

"Oh, my, yes," Mr. Howard said, lighting with excitement and admiration. "Yes, you will do perfectly. Arise, my dear."

Lady Farrah stood from her curtsy and gave Mr. Howard the most charming smile the buffoon was ever likely to have received.

"What did you tell him?" Angeline whispered to Melanie.

"That Lady Farrah had heard all about his financial prowess and come all this way to offer herself in marriage to him," Melanie whispered in return.

"That her family is one of the finest in London, and that they could improve his social standing to a degree that would give him status in addition to his wealth," Olive added. "Which is precisely why he came to the house party looking for a bride."

"And that she was eager to marry as quickly as possible," Melanie finished, "so he'd better propose soon."

"Places, everyone, places," Miss Julia called out, marching through the backstage area. "We have a play to perform, then, as I understand it, we have an announcement to be made." She looked directly at Angeline with an approving smile as she spoke.

"Lady Farrah, isn't it?" Mr. Howard went on with this whirlwind courtship as they all scrambled to take a copy of the script from a nearby table and make their way to the makeshift wings. "Let us spend as much time as possible between our duties as thespians discussing arrangements of another sort."

"I would like that, your grace," Lady Farrah said.

For the first time in the history of her involvement in theatrics, Angeline regretted that she had such a large part. Out of necessity, she was forced to spend most of her time for the next hour on the stage, whether she had lines or not. It was maddening to only be able to catch a glimpse of Mr. Howard and Lady Farrah during scene changes and shifts in the action. Every time she noticed them, however, they had inched closer and closer together. As true as it was that the whole thing was a ruse, the two did seem to get along quite well.

Even though Angeline wasn't privy to the action taking place behind the scenes, she was able to look out at the audience and see Rafe through the entire performance. That was all the prize she herself needed. Rafe seemed thoroughly diverted by the performance. He kept his hand in front of his mouth for most of her scenes—whether to stop himself from laughing or to hide his smile, which he couldn't seem to lose, now that she'd won it from him, she didn't know. All she knew was that she loved him. He was the perfect match for her, and whatever speech he'd made to Avery to convince him to allow the match, it must have been eloquent and magnificent. Avery sat by Rafe's side—and for some reason, Frank Crymble was there in the audience as well, watching Melanie, of all people—and even though Avery didn't look overjoyed, he did seem resigned.

At last, the play was over, and the entire cast took the stage for a bow. Including—much to Angeline's astonishment and joy—Lady Farrah, who held Mr. Howard's hand throughout the curtain call. Before the cast could go about their business, Miss Julia took the stage.

"Thank you for attending this afternoon's performance," she said with a beaming smile. "But before you go, Lord Rothbury and Lord Carnlough would like to make an announcement."

The assembly applauded in anticipation of that announcement as Rafe and Avery rose to take the stage. Lady Farrah narrowed her eyes at Rafe, then at Angeline, her expression going sour as she guessed what the announcement might be. Mr. Howard leaned in and whispered something to her that seemed to improve her countenance immensely, though.

"I will keep this brief," Avery said, with a bit of a sigh, once he reached the dais. "Lord Rothbury has asked for my sister, Lady Angeline's hand in marriage, and I have consented." Another round of applause rose up from the audience. "Furthermore," Avery went on, "I have agreed to allow them to marry this coming weekend, which Lord Rothbury has assured me is a sign of his good faith and intention to go through with the wedding—" he peeked anxiously to Lady Farrah, who had her chin so high in the air that Angeline thought a strong rain would drown her, "and not because it means anything else," Avery finished, glancing out at the audience, as if daring them to start rumors about reasons for haste.

Angeline blushed hot. "That wasn't necessary," she told Avery once he stepped back to her side.

"Considering the way I was manipulated into this match, I think it was," Avery said, feigning frustration. Angeline knew it was feigned. Avery's eyes sparkled too much for it to be otherwise. "And you're certain this is what you want?" he asked.

"I most certainly am," Angeline replied, hugging Rafe's arm.

"Then I'm happy for you," Avery sighed. "And in spite of my earlier reservations, I give you my blessing."

Angeline let go of Rafe's arm long enough to hug her brother. The joy spreading across the stage wasn't quite done yet, though.

"As I understand it, we have another announcement as well," Miss Julia went on.

"Indeed, we do," Mr. Howard went on, stepping forward and bringing Lady Farrah with him. "For I have just proposed to the lovely Lady Farrah Beauregard, and miracle of miracles, she has consented to become my wife."

Another round of applause followed. Lady Farrah preened and nodded and behaved as though she thought she were royalty.

"How lovely," Miss Julia said. "I would like to offer my deepest congratulations to the future Mr. and Mrs. Howard."

"*Mrs.* Howard?" Lady Farrah said, her jaw dropping.

"And I would like to announce that I plan to take my new bride on a luxurious, around the world, grand tour, booking all of the most luxurious hotels and resorts and traveling in the very first of first-classes on every ship," Mr. Howard added.

Lady Farrah blinked rapidly, her face coloring precipitously. Angeline thought the woman might be about to cry, but even if she were, she clung to Mr. Howard's arm so tightly that, in spite of everything, Angeline was confident she'd done the right thing. Not only had Mr. Howard promised her a tour of the world in style, he'd given her a way to have her love child while on that tour in such a way that no one back home would bat too much of an eyelash when they returned with a baby. As far as Angeline was concerned, Lady Farrah had gotten extraordinarily lucky. When the peevish woman sent Angeline a look as the applause died down and they all left the dais, Angeline was convinced Lady Farrah knew full well what kind of a favor Angeline had done for her.

"And now," Rafe murmured in Angeline's ear as the audience headed back to the house and the actors to the changing tents, "I think it's time we got you out of this silly costume."

"Do you intend to be my dresser, Lord Rothbury?" Angeline asked with a teasing grin.

"I intend to be your undresser," Rafe murmured against her ear. "Make an excuse and fetch your gown from the tent. Bring it back to your bedroom to change. I can guarantee you will like what you find there once you return."

"Oh?" Angeline gasped.

Rafe's answer was a wicked wink before he turned and walked off, heading swiftly back to the house.

"Oh!" Angeline giggled, turning and running for the tent.

She ducked and dodged her fellow actors, pushing past people without a heed for their safety, in order to fetch the clothes she'd arrived at the tent wearing before the performance. They were hung neatly on a rack attended by one of Miss Julia's servants, but Angeline grabbed them and crushed them against her chest before dodging and stumbling her way back out of the tent.

"And just where are you going in such a hurry?" Melanie asked as Angeline zipped past her conversing with Mr. Crymble outside of the ladies' tent.

"Back to my room," Angeline said breathlessly. "I've been given to understand there's a treat waiting there for me." She hurried on, then paused and turned back, saying, "I might be a tad late to supper."

Melanie laughed. "I'll make your excuses."

"I'll return the favor, if you need it," Angeline said before speeding on. That was what friends were for, after all. They helped each other get into trouble, and they helped each other stay out of it as well.

Angeline had an idea of what to expect once she returned to her room, but what she actually found was so glorious it made her laugh out loud. Rafe was already in her bed, completely nude, and stretched out like some sort of recumbent, Roman god. He had the bedcovers thrown back as well, and every line of his impressive physique was on display, including a particularly stiff and proud line.

"What would you have done if a maid had entered the room instead of me?" she asked in a whisper, locking her bedroom door behind her and scurrying to the bed. She threw her clothes clumsily on the chair by her fireplace, ignoring them when they dropped to the floor, and went straight to work unfastening her toga.

"I would have been extraordinarily embarrassed," Rafe said, continuing to lounge as he watched her undress, hunger in his eyes. "But I wagered that most, if not all, of the maids would be busy helping deconstruct the impromptu stage or helping ladies change out of their sheets, and the likelihood of any of them being upstairs at all was slim."

"I think you're right," Angeline said, slithering out of her costume. She thanked the Romans profusely for the simplicity of their style of dress as she stepped over the folds of fabric pooled around her feet and launched herself toward the bed. "You really are lovely to look at, you know," she gasped, climbing onto the bed and straddling his thighs so that she could gaze down at him.

"I was just thinking the same thing about you," Rafe growled, raking his hands over her thighs as they braced on either side of him. "Though I have one complaint."

Angeline's heart skipped an anxious beat. "Oh?" she asked, glancing down at herself and wondering where she'd gone wrong.

"For a sweet, innocent, blushing maiden, you are

unbelievably bold," he said, fire in his eyes and teasing on his lips. "No virgin I can think of would rush into a position like the one you're in now."

"As you will recall from last night's activities," Angeline said with pretend haughtiness, "I am no longer a virgin."

"I do recall," Rafe said in an equally jokey voice.

"And why should I be shy or reticent with the man I intend to spend the rest of my life loving?" she asked on, leaning forward so that she could stroke his chest, loving the way his chest hair tickled her hands. "Unless you would prefer me to tremble and faint at your touch." She bent over all the way and closed her mouth over his in a kiss.

She didn't really think she knew what she was doing where kissing was concerned, but Rafe knew. It was easy to kiss a man who was so good at it himself and to learn what she needed to know from him. He brushed his hands over her back in a way that had her breaking out in gooseflesh as she kissed him, and when he brought those hands down to her bum to squeeze and knead her, she thought she might melt right into him with need.

"I want you inside of me," she murmured, feeling deliciously sultry and wicked. "Like you were last night. That felt so much better than I thought it would, and now I can't think of anything else."

Rather than rushing to do as she wanted immediately, Rafe slipped a hand between her legs to tease and please the part of her that ached for him. "You're certainly wet enough to want me," he said in a deep, growling voice that made Angeline shiver.

Or perhaps it was the way his hand delved into her, almost but not quite satisfying the need that pulsed through her. She'd never dreamed that a man's touch that way could feel so good, and as he explored her, she found herself moving against him, seeking out her own pleasure. She tried to kiss him at the same time, but didn't quite have the coordination to manage it. Instead, she focused on rubbing herself against his hand and cooing with pleasure as she did.

"My God, Angel, you're a wanton," Rafe said breathlessly, helping her along. "I will exist in a place of perpetual exhaustion for the whole of our married life."

Angeline could only respond with a needy sigh as the coil of pleasure tightened within her. She needed him so desperately, but wasn't certain what to do about it. Blessedly, Rafe helped her along, grasping himself and holding himself up, then guiding her to bear down on him. The feeling of bringing him into her body by her own choice and on her own power was so perfect that her body erupted into orgasm right then. He encouraged her to continue to move, though, and as she did, her orgasm extended and consumed her. She rode him like everything in the world depended on it, crying out in time to his thrusts.

"Angeline," Rafe moaned, bucking his hips into her even after her waves of pleasure faded. "Angeline." He gripped her hips hard, then let out a beautiful, animalistic cry as warmth spread through her. It was miraculous. Angeline didn't think she would ever feel as though their mating was anything less.

She'd won. That much was as evident as the heat and sweat of their bodies as they relaxed and flopped together on the bed. She'd won the grandest prize that the house party—and life in general—could promise her.

"I love you so," she hummed happily, closing her eyes as she nestled against Rafe's chest.

"And I love you, my angel," he said. "I always will."

EPILOGUE

When Angeline knocked on the open door to Olive's L'arbre's room, Olive barely heard it. She was far too engrossed—and excited—in the scientific journal in her hands.

"Yoohoo, this is reality calling Olive! Are you ready?"

"Hmm?" Olive jerked her attention away from the contents page and glanced at her friend. "Oh, yes. I'm dressed."

Angeline's knowing gaze swept Olive, who tried not to feel self-conscious. "Yes, you always look lovely in blue, Olive dear. But are you *ready*? You're clutching at that journal as if you would much rather spend the evening reading than dancing."

With a slight huff, Olive rolled her eyes and planted one fist on her hip. "Of *course* I'd rather spend the evening reading than dancing. Anyone with half a brain would rather spend the evening reading than dancing."

143

Angeline was already halfway across the room, reaching for Olive's hand, when she giggled. "Not me. And if *you* had a certain gentleman waiting to dance with you downstairs, you wouldn't either."

"Wouldn't what?"

"Wouldn't want to read instead of dance." Angeline gave her hand a tug. "Come *on*! We're all meeting in Melanie's room before heading downstairs."

Olive hesitated. It wasn't that she didn't love her friends dearly, and want to spend time with them...it was that a new issue of the Journal of the Society of Archaeology was only released once a quarter, and this one was sure to contain the thrilling climax to the latest of Aberdeen Jones's thrilling *Adventures*.

"What's going on in here? Are we no' meeting in Melanie's room?" Their friend Raina Prince stuck her head around the doorframe. "Or are we meeting here?"

"No, no, we're on our way there." Angeline flapped her hand in Raina's direction. "As soon as I can convince Olive here that we're more important than her journal."

Olive gasped and clutched the bundle of papers to her chest. "I *know* that. You think I don't know what's important?"

The sparkle in Angeline's eyes betrayed her teasing, as Raina huffed in impatience. "Then *bring* the journal, ye wee scholar. My brother was always reading at the dinner table too, ye ken."

Brother?

The mere word weakened Olive's resolve, and the

next thing she knew, Angeline was tugging her out the door. Olive stumbled along, the journal clutched to her chest, as her cheerful friend asked the question she longed to ask.

"You have three brothers, Raina dear. Which one do you mean?"

Raina shot a teasing glance over her shoulder. "Why, Phineas, of course. He's the intellectual one in the family. I always thought he and Olive would get along swimmingly."

Phineas Prince.

Olive prided herself on her sharp wit and brain. So how come, when *his* name was mentioned, her mind seemed to turn into a big pink ball of mush, and her *body* seemed to take over? All these inconvenient urges and flutters...

"Get along swimmingly?" Angeline repeated, tugging Olive down the corridor. "What, like wearing uncomfortable clothes and holding your breath and getting salt water up your nose?"

As they reached Melanie's door, Raina winked. "Only if you're doing it wrong."

"Is this an analogy?" Angeline hissed at Olive as their friend slipped in to join the rest. "You know I've never been good at analogies."

Olive, her mind on the idea of *Phineas* in a swimming costume, managed to murmur, "A metaphor, perhaps."

Angeline clucked her tongue good-naturedly and pulled them both into the room. "Well, school is over, and we're able to enjoy one another without having to study for silly grammar tests. Sit down and read your journal until the rest of us are ready."

Olive hurried toward a chair and sank down grate-fully, holding the journal in front of her like a shield as she glanced around at their friends, who were all primping and taking care of last-minute touches to their toilette before this evening's entertainment.

She loved them, really she did, and she was beyond grateful to be here with them.

But sometimes, a girl needed her archaeological fix...

Exhaling, Olive opened the journal to the begin-ning of Aberdeen Jones's *Adventure* and tried to concentrate.

But the thought of a certain Scotsman, his long legs encased in a dashing kilt, kept intruding...

———

THANK YOU SO MUCH FOR READING ANGELINE AND Rafe's story! Are you ready to read more? *The Scholar and the Scot*, by Caroline Lee is the next book up in the series! I bet you just can't wait to read Olive and Phineas's story! You can find The Scholar and the Scot here!

AND DO YOU WANT TO KNOW MORE ABOUT ANGELINE and Avery's family? You can read all about That Wicked

O'Shea Family, starting with *I Kissed an Earl* (*and I Liked It*)....

LADY MARIE O'SHEA LIVES LIFE BY HER OWN rules...

BUT HER DAYS OF RUNNING FREE END WHEN HER brother, Lord Fergus O'Shea, returns from England, intent on marrying his sisters off to keep them from being the scourge of the county. And when Marie lands herself in a scandalous amount of trouble, she ends up as the first sister doomed to whatever marriage of convenience her brother can arrange.

BAD BOY CHRISTIAN DARROW IS HAVING TOO MUCH fun to be tied down...

AND AS THE YOUNGER SON OF AN EARL, HE ISN'T expected to amount to much. Which is why playing pranks and getting into trouble with Marie the moment they meet is his idea of a good time. Sparks fly between him and Marie and the scandal is totally worth the risk...

...UNTIL ONE PRANK GOES TOO FAR.

.   .   .

Can Marie save Christian from the consequences of what was supposed to be a bit of fun? Or will a twist of fate prove that life is more serious than either Marie or Christian ever expected?

A friends to lovers romance that will make you laugh and cry.

PLEASE BE ADVISED: Steam level – very spicy!

If you enjoyed this book and would like to hear more from me, please sign up for my newsletter! When you sign up, you'll get a free, full-length novella, A Passionate Deception. Victorian identity theft has never been so exciting in this story of hope, tricks, and starting over. Part of my West Meets East series, A Passionate Deception can be read as a stand-alone. Pick up your free copy today by signing up to receive my newsletter (which I only send out when I have a new release)!

Sign up here: http://eepurl.com/cbaVMH

.   .   .

ARE YOU ON SOCIAL MEDIA? I AM! COME AND JOIN the fun on Facebook: http://www.facebook.com/merryfarmerreaders

I'M ALSO A HUGE FAN OF INSTAGRAM AND POST LOTS of original content there: https://www.instagram.com/merryfarmer/

Click here for a complete list of other works by Merry Farmer.

ABOUT THE AUTHOR

I hope you have enjoyed *The Angel and the Aristocrat*. If you'd like to be the first to learn about when new books in the series come out and more, please sign up for my news-letter here: http://eepurl.com/cbaVMH And remember, Read it, Review it, Share it! For a complete list of works by Merry Farmer with links, please visit http://wp.me/P5ttjb-14F.

Merry Farmer is an award-winning novelist who lives in suburban Philadelphia with her cats, Torpedo, her grumpy old man, and Justine, her hyperactive new baby. She has been writing since she was ten years old and real-ized one day that she didn't have to wait for the teacher to assign a creative writing project to write something. It was the best day of her life. She then went on to earn not one but two degrees in History so that she would always have something to write about. Her books have reached the Top 100 at Amazon, iBooks, and Barnes & Noble, and have been named finalists in the prestigious RONE and Rom Com Reader's Crown awards.

ACKNOWLEDGMENTS

I owe a huge debt of gratitude to my awesome beta-readers, Caroline Lee and Jolene Stewart, for their suggestions and advice. And double thanks to Julie Tague, for being a truly excellent editor and to Cindy Jackson for being an awesome assistant!

Click here for a complete list of other works by Merry Farmer.

Printed in Great Britain
by Amazon